I AM ISABELLA

It seems an innocent enough deception — pretend to be the absent heiress, Isabella Hale, just for one evening. And certainly the objective is a noble one — to present a generous check to an unquestionably deserving charity. As it turns out, however, Carol Andrews' identity is not the only thing that isn't all it seems. In no time at all, she finds herself in a high-stakes game of deceit and danger, in which she faces the ultimate penalty — death . . .

PP 12/04/19

SH
HM
MC

V. J. BANIS

I AM ISABELLA

Complete and Unabridged

LINFORD
Leicester

First published in Great Britain

First Linford Edition
published 2013

A catalogue record for *this* book is available
from the British Library.

ISBN 978–1–4448–1796–6

Published by
F. A. Thorpe (Publishing)
Anstey, Leicestershire

Set by Words & Graphics Ltd.
Anstey, Leicestershire
Printed and bound in Great Britain by
T. J. International Ltd., Padstow, Cornwall

This book is printed on acid-free paper

1

Hale House stood apart, surveying its kingdom. The road cut a mostly straight path through the hills, past forests, and finally veered, rising steeply upward to the house. The driver of the car took the final sharp curve a little too fast and the car slipped sideways a bit before he righted it.

The young woman in the rear seat started to say something, hesitated, and changed her mind, leaning back in the seat. *Better not rock the boat*, she told herself. It was better to remain quiet until she was surer of things, a little more confident how to act.

She was strikingly pretty, even in the dim light. The driver, a brutish man with intense dark eyes, glanced back at her several times in the mirror, his glances blatantly lustful.

Her hair, in daylight a pale yellow shade, looked silvery in the car's interior.

She had a fine bone structure beneath the fair skin — the high cheekbones, the strong chin-line. Her mouth, painted a tangerine shade, was a little too full to be truly beautiful, but it gave her an odd pouting look, and her eyes were vivid green and wide set.

The driver had noticed her figure too. It would probably go to fat when she got to middle age, but for now it was generous of curve and appealing, the kind of soft femininity he liked in a woman. But if she had any awareness of him she had not shown it. *Bitch*, he thought sourly.

He had also noticed that she looked nervous. Which wasn't particularly surprising, he told himself.

The house was bright with lights, gleaming from either side of the massive carved door, shining along the driveway and spilling from every window.

The chauffeur stopped the car just by the steps up to the door. She reached for the door handle without thinking, checked herself, and waited instead for him to open the door for her. She saw his approving glance at her legs as he helped her out and though she thought him unattractive, it gave her confidence a boost.

She needed all the confidence she could summon. She hadn't counted on their coming out to meet her, a crowd of people. She had thought there would be time to settle in, compose herself, before it really began in earnest, but the door of the house opened before the driver had even released her arm and there was Wilfred advancing to greet her, carrying his martini with him.

His wife Minnie waited in the open doorway and smiled a toothy smile. Behind her, seeming from below to fill the entry hall, were others who were strangers. She looked up, saw them all looking at her, and smiled broadly.

'Wilfred, hello,' she greeted him and came quickly up the steps toward where he stood.

He met her halfway, embracing her and kissing her cheek soundly. 'You look wonderful,' he said. 'Welcome home.'

The group on the porch could not see

the mischievous smile she gave him. 'I should,' she said for him alone to hear, 'I'm wearing somewhere around fifty thousand dollars.'

He glowered at her, but again so that the others would not see. When he turned toward them, piloting her up the stairs in a paternal manner, he was once again beaming.

She held out her hand as she neared the top. 'Minnie, how wonderful to see you again, darling.'

Minnie took the proffered hand and leaned closer to kiss her. 'Isabella, honey, I am so glad you're here at last. Everybody has been on pins and needles waiting for you to arrive.'

Wilfred turned the young woman in another direction, saying, 'Isabella, this is our guest of honor, Dr. Everson. Dr. Everson, may I introduce my niece, Isabella Hale.'

There were nearly a dozen more waiting to be personally introduced. She met them all with the same fixed smile, a handshake and a how-do-you-do. After the doctor, the people she was meeting became a blur of faces and names and hands thrust into hers. There would be time enough later to sort them out, though. Anyway, it was common knowledge that she was bad with names, so that was no problem.

'You'll want to go up to your room and freshen up a bit,' Wilfred said.

'Yes, I think I had better,' she said with a little laugh. 'I feel as if I'd made the entire trip by car instead of just the last leg.'

'There is a closer airport, you know,' Wilfred chided her.

He had explained to her earlier on that this was an argument they had been through often before. 'Yes, I know,' she said, 'if I wanted to fly in those half-engined things that cross the mountains in little hops and jumps. No, thank you, I would rather do the last seventy or eighty miles in a car. And that's what a chauffeur is for, is it not? Excuse me, everyone, please. I'll be down in a few minutes.'

She started toward the wide stairs that split the hall in half. Minnie moved as if to accompany her but the young woman waved her off. 'No, don't bother,' she said. 'See that the guests are entertained, please. I'll be all right.'

Already, in early September, the upper New York State air was cool. She tugged free her dark burgundy scarf as she went up, and let it trail on the pale pink carpeting.

At the landing she went to the right with no hesitation, followed the stairs to the second floor, and went straight to the door of the room that would be ready for her.

Her bags had already been brought up in that moment or two that she had spent being introduced to the guests. Clearly, things went like clockwork here at Hale House. The maid had not yet come along to unpack them but she would almost certainly be here any minute now.

That was one of the things to bear in mind in the next twenty-four hours, one of the drawbacks of living in a house like this, with all of this wealth and Lord-alone-knew how many kinds of servants. You could not count on being alone for more than a minute or two, could never know when a maid would appear, or the housekeeper, or someone or other.

She would have liked right now to let her guard down, if only for a few minutes, to relax, just to be herself briefly before she had to resume playing a part before the audience waiting for her downstairs.

She could not do that, of course, because the maid would be coming in any minute to begin unpacking her things.

She threw her coat carelessly on the bed, consistent with the manner she had adopted for the evening. The coat was leopard, the real thing. It accounted for a large portion of the fifty thousand dollars she had mentioned to Wilfred. The diamonds and emeralds in a cluster at her throat accounted for most of the rest. Her suit was a Chanel, very simple and very elegant. And expensive.

She saw her image in the mirror and smiled approvingly. So this is what it feels like to be worth millions, she told herself.

She frowned, thinking back to the scene at the door and the various people she had met. She could not help wondering if any of them had realized, or even suspected, that she was not Isabella Hale.

★   ★   ★

Less than three weeks before, she had been Carol Andrews, and if she had been wearing a leopard coat, it would have been because she was modeling it for a photographic assignment.

Which was unlikely. The fact was, she was not very successful as a model. The full blown, generously curved figure that made her so attractive to men was a very different thing from the stark thinness required of a successful model. Despite her best efforts, no amount of dieting could give her the pencil-straight sleekness of those glamorous creatures.

When she had first entered the field she had consoled herself that her 'big break' was just on the horizon and that she would soon be past the meager assignments and scrimped living. She was nineteen at the time, confident, and determined to be a cover-girl model.

By the time she was twenty, she was a bit discouraged, but she kept on.

By the time she had turned twenty-one, just a little over a month ago, she had faced the bitter truth. She was never going to make it as a model. Her fresh youthfulness had so far seen her through and gotten her enough assignments to meet her expenses, but even those jobs were fading as her youth faded. She was no longer suited for the role of pink-cheeked schoolgirl. Putting it to herself in the cruelest possible terms, she was on the verge of being washed up.

It was at this crucial juncture that Wilfred and Minnie Hale had appeared in her life.

The interview her agent had arranged for her brought her to the Sherry Netherland Hotel, to the tower suite, one of the most elegant of the city's accommodations. She had arrived promptly and a little uneasy. Interviews in hotel rooms were not uncommon, but she'd had one or two unpleasant experiences with gentlemen who had mistaken ideas about models and their interests. Nor did the undeniable elegance of the hotel completely assuage her worries. Money did not necessarily guarantee morals or even good manners.

She stopped at the desk, as instructed, giving her name, and a call was made to the suite to tell the guests she was on her way up. Guests in the Sherry's tower suite did not welcome surprise visitors.

She had no sooner stepped off the elevator than the door to the suite opened and a man appeared. He was tall and thin, with a neatly trimmed moustache and he carried a martini, although it was just three o'clock in the afternoon. Instinctively, she did not like him, though she could not have said why.

'Miss Andrews?' A carefully plucked eyebrow tilted upward.

'Yes.' She gave him a professional smile.

'Come in, please.' He held the door wide, moving aside for her.

A flight of stairs went up from the tiled foyer, presumably. The sitting room was to her left. Through the window across the room she had a quick glimpse of the New York skyline. She had always wanted to live like this, in an elegant penthouse overlooking the city.

'I'm Wilfred Hale,' he said. 'And this is my wife, Minnie.'

'How do you do.' Minnie did not rise from the green silk sofa to greet her but her smile seemed genuine and her look was interested. She had the appearance of a big woman who had shrunk. She looked, too, as if there were a lot she wanted to say, and would if encouraged at all. The color of her expensive dress clashed with the sofa on which she was sitting. Carol thought it always would. Money did not guarantee taste, either.

'I confess, I am not exactly sure of the right . . . er . . . right form in interviewing a model,' Mr. Hale said, and looked her up and down as if he might be considering a price per pound.

'Perhaps if I knew what kind of modeling you had in mind,' Carol suggested. Her agent had told her only that the prospective client wanted a blonde, of her general type and age, and was willing to pay top dollar.

'We should see how she walks,' Minnie

said. 'And how she sits. That's important.'

'Yes, of course.' Mr. Hale gave his wife a smile like a pat on the head. 'Would you mind, Miss . . . ?'

'Andrews, Carol Andrews.'

'Perhaps without your coat.'

She slipped off her coat and walked from one end of the room to the other, turning gracefully. She registered that they had evaded her question about the kind of modeling they wanted. She sat obediently and stood. They seemed pleased with what they saw.

Mr. Hale finished his drink. He looked toward a tray of bottles on one table, but apparently decided against mixing another.

'Tell me a little about yourself,' he said. 'Your background. Where you come from, that sort of thing. Are you married?'

'Mr. Hale . . . '

'Call me Wilfred, please. I want us to be friends.'

Mentally she gritted her teeth. 'I think perhaps it would be best if we got clear between us just what sort of job you had in mind. My agent was a bit vague . . . '

'In due time,' he said. Seeing her

annoyance, he added, smiling, 'Will you feel better if I assure you no one is going to ask you to remove your clothes?'

She smiled in response and relaxed a little. Every model sooner or later got offers to do 'specialty shots'.

'I'm afraid there's very little background to tell,' she said. 'My father was a doctor. My mother died when I was quite young, my father three years ago. I am single. I came to New York two years ago to be a model.'

'And you've succeeded,' he said, but in a tone of voice that made it more of a question than a statement.

★ ★ ★

Wilfred Hale was filling in the blanks she had left. Her father had been, not rich, he already knew that, but fairly well off — she had an unmistakable air of breeding. She had been to good schools. Probably she'd had a year in a finishing school. Zurich, he guessed. There was a certain posture, a certain way of sitting and standing, of carrying oneself, that one only got from schools of that sort.

'Have you done much traveling?' he asked, lighting a cigarette, which he took from a gold case. He did not offer one to his wife or to Carol.

'I spent a year in Switzerland, in a finishing school,' she said. 'And a week in Rome, on holiday, and another in Paris. I'm afraid that's it.'

'Have you ever done any acting?'

Carol's mind was working fast. Acting? Might he be a producer? But why go through a modeling agency for an actress? 'No,' she said. 'Oh, I did a television commercial for a kitchen cleanser. I wasn't very good, I'm afraid. They said I didn't look at all like a housewife.'

'That's good,' he said, without explaining why he should think that. He changed his mind about the martini and went to mix himself another one.

Mrs. Hale leaned forward slightly. She had a way of sitting that was particularly ungraceful, with her ankles crossed and her knees apart. She had been studying Carol intently while her husband conducted the interview.

'Does our name mean anything to you?' she asked.

Carol hesitated briefly. Hale? Had she committed some faux pas by not recognizing them?

'I'm afraid not,' she shook her head. 'But I must confess, I'm terribly bad with names.'

Mrs. Hale laughed loudly. 'So is Isabella,' she said to her husband. 'That's a sign, I'd say.'

He looked displeased at her remark. 'Coincidence, I think,' he said.

Something flickered at the back of Carol's consciousness. Isabella. Isabella Hale? The name was familiar, but she could not quite place it.

Wilfred came back with a fresh martini, and took charge again. 'Please, sit down, Miss . . . ?' he hesitated.

'Andrews,' she told him again. Isabella was not the only one who was bad with names. She sat in one of the French chairs. He sat in the other, the two of them flanking Minnie on the sofa, so that she had to continually turn her head from side to side to watch them both.

'You don't recognize the name Isabella Hale?' he asked.

'I'm afraid not,' she said.

'She's one of the richest women in the world,' Minnie said. She watched Carol for her reaction and so missed the disapproving look her husband gave her.

It clicked then in Carol's mind. Isabella Hale, the heiress. Hale coffees and teas.

'I do recall, vaguely . . . ' she said. 'The press called her . . . '

'A madcap heiress,' he supplied with a chagrined smile.

She remembered now. And somewhere in the past there had been a scandal, hadn't there? After which she had rather disappeared from the news.

'Isabella Hale is my niece, my late brother's child,' he said. 'Besides being her uncle and her friend, I also manage her fortune for her. When my brother passed away, I was trustee of the estate. She was quite a young woman, so everything went into a trust for her until she came of age. When she did, she chose to let me continue to manage her affairs. I have her full power of attorney, you

16

understand, and full authority to represent her. Also to handle her money matters as I see fit. I mention these facts so there will be no misunderstanding about the proposition I am about to make you.'

He turned to his wife. 'Have you the photograph?' he asked.

She handed him a large manila envelope. He removed a photograph from it, handing the picture to Carol.

Carol found herself looking at a studio portrait of a girl in her teens, into a pair of clearly haughty eyes. The girl was blonde and not unattractive, although her attractiveness was due more to the *joie de vivre* she projected rather than to the arrangement of her features.

'My niece,' Mr. Hale said.

'She's very pretty.' Carol handed the photograph back. 'But, really, Mr. Hale . . . '

'Wilfred,' he said, in a voice that struck her as a bit too emphatic.

' . . . I don't see . . . '

'We want you to become Isabella Hale.'

For a moment she could only sit and stare in stunned silence. Then rising, she said, 'I'm afraid this is not in my line of work. Perhaps if you tried an acting school . . . '

'Miss Andrews,' he said, standing also, 'we are not engaging you to take part in some illegal scheme.'

'I haven't suggested that you were.'

'You've been suggesting exactly that since you came into the room,' he said, smiling.

And I will remember in the future not to underestimate you, she said silently — *that retiring manner is only a mask.*

'What we want of you,' he went on, 'is not only perfectly legal, but for a very good cause as well. If you will only let me explain further . . . '

'It's for charity,' Mrs. Hale interjected, earning her another disapproving look from her husband.

'Won't you wait until you hear what I want before you turn me down?' he asked Carol.

'Even if what you say is true,' she said, softening a little, 'I'm afraid I'm still not the one you want. For one thing, your niece and I look nothing alike.'

'But there you are mistaken,' he said.

'That picture is years old,' Mrs. Hale said quickly.

'My wife is right. I should have explained that when I showed it to you. It was taken several years ago, when Isabella was just sixteen. She is twenty-two now. You're about that, aren't you?'

'Twenty-one. But even allowing for that, there still isn't any real resemblance between us.'

'There is quite enough resemblance for our purposes. You are about the same age, the same general height and build. You are both blonde. You walk and move as if you had breeding, a finishing school background, which you tell me is so. You could easily be from Isabella's social class.'

'But those things aren't enough to carry off an impersonation. Our faces are quite different. I have high cheekbones, her face is round.'

'Baby fat.'

'No one could ever mistake one of us for the other.'

'They could if they did not know my

niece and had never seen her,' Mr. Hale said.

'But there are photographs, newspaper pictures . . . '

He shook his head, smiling. 'My niece has been traveling for the last several years. There was some difficulty in her teens, about the time that picture was taken — oh, nothing concerned with the business at hand. She went abroad. Not to the fashionable places, but out-of-the-way spots. A missionary colony in Africa, a refugee center in Bangladesh. The sort of places, I am trying to say, where there are no society editors. And she has been assiduous in all this time in avoiding the press, and photographers in general. To the best of my knowledge, this was the last photograph of her that appeared in the newspapers, more than five years ago.'

He took a clipping from the manila envelope and handed it to her. Carol unfolded it and looked at the photograph. There was not much to see. It showed a blonde woman getting off an airplane, but that was about as much as one could say about it. It had obviously been taken from a considerable distance, probably with a telescopic lens. The young woman's face was blurred and virtually indistinguishable. She wore a loose-fitting raincoat that let you see only that she was reasonably slim. It might have been Carol Andrews herself instead of Isabella Hale — or for that matter any one of thousands of other young women.

She sat down again, slowly. 'Explain to me fully what you want,' she said, meeting his gaze evenly. 'I won't promise that I will agree to anything. Just so we understand one another, I won't even promise, in fact, that I won't go to the police about it if this smells at all funny.'

'Fair enough.' he sat too, looking amused more than concerned by the threat.

Mrs. Hale too grinned and leaned back. 'You are going to be tickled pink when you hear what we want,' she said, 'I guarantee it.'

Her husband ignored that comment. 'For several years now,' he began, 'my niece has been interested in children. Orphans, refugees, the needy. Most of her travel has been in line with this interest. That missionary colony in Africa that I mentioned works with abandoned children, you see, and that is one of her pet projects. Another of her interests, far more recent, has been a group called The World's Children Foundation. Have you heard of it?'

Carol nodded. 'I believe so.'

'It's rather a new organization. A foundation devoted to needy children throughout the world. Its headquarters are right here in New York.'

He paused, sipping his drink.

'As you can imagine,' he went on, 'Isabella has been out of touch with things here, traveling as she has been. It was only recently that she heard of The World's Children Foundation. When she did, she wrote to ask me about them. I gathered what information I could and sent it to her — I'm making this as short as I can, you understand, I don't want you to bolt before I have finished.'

Carol smiled despite herself.

'Isabella decided she wanted to make a contribution to the Foundation. A very sizable contribution, frankly.'

'A million dollars,' Mrs. Hale said.

Carol was appropriately impressed. 'I'd say that's very sizable.'

'Yes,' Mr. Hale said. 'Sizable enough that in fact, being perhaps a bit presumptuous, I made a big thing out of it. I arranged for a lavish dinner at our country estate, at which the check would be presented with a certain amount of fanfare. I notified the press, invited a number of important people — in short, the works. I expected my niece to be here, to make the presentation. But a few days ago I got an e-mail from her. She is not coming.'

He spread his hands palm up in a gesture of defeat. 'So, you see, I was left with egg on my face. I will look foolish, to say the least. The directors of the foundation, having been led to believe my niece is making the presentation, may be insulted. The press will have a field day. A perfectly generous gesture on my niece's part will be turned into a three ring circus. That madcap heiress title is sure to pop up again, a label she has spent years trying to live down. The sad truth is, the bad press will tarnish any good publicity that might come from her donation.'

He paused and gave her a significant look. 'Unless, that is, I find someone to take Isabella's place.'

'But, I . . . '

He quickly cut off her objections. 'As I have said already, none of these people, the ones who will be there for the presentation, know her. So far as I have been able to determine, none has ever met her. If so, it would be well in the past. At the most, they will have seen pictures of her in her teens, and those badly reproduced in newspapers. And it's important that you grasp the significance of this, they will be expecting Isabella Hale. They would accept you as my niece because they will be told that is who you are. They would have no reason to suspect otherwise.'

For a moment they were all silent. Carol was thinking, it sounded logical enough, even easy enough. Still she hesitated.

'We are prepared to pay you generously,' he went on. 'This dinner is to take place at Isabella's country estate, Hale House. You would have to travel there, only overnight, of course. We thought something in the neighborhood of ten thousand dollars might be satisfactory pay for the job.'

'I'd say it was very generous,' Carol said, 'if I were taking the job. But I'm afraid I still don't think . . . '

'Let us be very blunt with one another,' he said, speaking softly but intensely. 'You're hesitating because you think we are up to something, some scheme to cheat my niece out of some money, isn't that right?' Mrs. Hale chuckled.

'It had crossed my mind.'

'But I tell you quite plainly, I don't need Isabella there, or an impersonator either, to give away the money. I have full authority to do as I wish with the money. But, even setting that aside, say at the very worst I am stealing a million dollars from my niece, not for myself but to give it to the foundation. She can afford it. And it is going to a very worthy cause. You know that the foundation is legitimate and if you have any questions you can easily satisfy yourself on that score. You yourself will handle the check, see it, give it away. Even if I were doing this without my niece's blessing, and I am not, it would not be such a heinous crime, would it? A million dollars, to help children in need.'

Carol had never encountered anything like this before. Her instincts were to shy away from it. Yet, everything he said was reasonable.

At the very worst, when the time came, if there was anything that did not agree with what he had told her, she could expose him as a thief. If she agreed to do what he asked, she would insist upon seeing the check, and if she did not, or if it were not what he said, she could certainly put a stop to it then. There would be other people around. She had only to tell them the truth.

And, if the money really were going to The World's Children Foundation, then there was truly no harm in doing what he wanted.

'I need time to think this over,' she said.

'I'm afraid there's very little time to spare. We've less than three weeks in which to coach whomever we select.'

'But if no one knows her . . . ?'

'She must still know things Isabella would know. Where she's been in the last several years, her birthday, things about Minnie and myself, and about Hale House. So you see, time is of the essence.'

'It wouldn't be hard work,' Minnie said. 'And you'll like Hale House. It's a lovely place.'

Carol got up and went to the window, looking down. Fifth Avenue was a thin line upon which cars, little more than specks like ants, crawled.

Ten thousand dollars. She needed the money. She had scarcely enough in her checking account to cover her next rent payment. She had nothing set up in the way of work. It all sounded easy and above-board. Surely there was no moral wrong done in helping give a large sum of money to a worthy charity?

'Very well,' she said, taking a deep breath. 'I'll be Isabella Hale, for one night. I'll give away your million dollars.'

2

'Miss Hale?'

She turned, cursing herself silently for forgetting that she was now Isabella Hale and not Carol Andrews.

A young woman in a maid's uniform stood just inside the door, looking a little frightened (*so am I, dear heart*, Carol thought).

'Yes?'

She had nothing to fear from the servants, however.

'There's Mrs. Green, the housekeeper,' Wilfred had explained, 'and Harley's the butler. They, and the chauffeur, McCullogh, know who you really are. The rest of the servants will all be temporary people from town, hired just for the occasion. None of them have set eyes on Isabella before.'

Hale House was not often in use. Even before her voluntary exile, Isabella had not been fond of the place. It was too removed from the social mainstream, her preoccupation then. She had lived most of her time at her apartment on Park Avenue in Manhattan.

'Shall I unpack for you?' the maid asked.

'Please do.' Carol turned her back as if the maid were of no consequence. She would have liked to chat with the frightened young thing, to put both of them at their ease, would have been just as happy to do her own unpacking.

She had to act as Isabella would act, however. She turned her back, fussing with her hair in the mirror. She sniffed at a perfume atomizer atop the dresser — Chanel — and gave herself a quick misting, touched up her lips. As she was putting the lipstick back, she saw her cell phone in the purse. She had forgotten that. It didn't get much use, but it would not do to have someone call Carol Andrews while she was downstairs impersonating Isabella Hale. She left the phone atop the dresser.

She had delayed as long as she could. It was time to go down. She had butterflies in her stomach.

The maid, her arms filled with dresses, looked shyly at her as Carol turned. Carol gave her a genuinely warm smile and was rewarded with one in return. She left the room and started downstairs.

Wilfred had taken his guests into the large drawing room. Carol felt, walking into it, as the early Christians must have felt stepping into the arena.

'There's nothing to be afraid of,' she told herself. 'No one is going to guess. No one is even going to suspect.'

'Here's my little girl,' Wilfred said, coming to her side. She found his manner grating, but she beamed at him as if she were really fond of him and joined the circle of guests, all eager to converse with her.

Because everyone wanted to chat with her, none of them truly did. She had to keep up a flow of small talk, cocktail party chatter in which there was little if any danger of giving away her secret.

Because she was playing a part and Wilfred and Minnie had given her this clue, she was friendly and charming, without being too friendly or too charming. She was patronizing because she was a patron. She had known enough people like Isabella Hale to know how to act. She found it distasteful. However, she had not cared for the grinning clucking housewife she had portrayed in the cleanser commercial for television, either. She looked upon this in the same light.

Wilfred stayed close to her and whenever he left her, Minnie materialized at her other elbow. They must have rehearsed this very carefully.

She found herself once again with Dr. Everson. By now, Carol knew he was the director of The World's Children Foundation, and the man to whom a bit later she would be giving Isabella's money.

'Are you enjoying yourself, Doctor?' she asked, the good hostess.

'Very much,' he said. 'You have a beautiful place here.' His porcine eyes made a sweep of the room, as if appraising the value of the furnishings.

'Where's that nice young man of yours?' Minnie wanted to know. 'Wasn't he supposed to be here, too?'

The doctor frowned. 'Yes, he was,' he

said, his eyes once again moving about the room in search of the young man in question. 'As a matter of fact, he made rather a thing out of being permitted to accompany me, and now he's late.'

'Perhaps he decided that philanthropic dinners were not exciting enough for him,' Carol said. 'If he's as young as you suggest . . . '

'Here he is now,' Dr. Everson said, interrupting her and looking past her.

Carol turned in that direction. A young man was walking toward them across the crowded room. Her first thought was that he was not so young as their remarks had led her to believe. The man walking purposefully across the room was closer to thirty.

He was good looking, with a rugged, squarish face. The cocktail crowd seemed to part before him as if by magic, and Carol found herself thinking she would not want to be in his way, in any sense.

Their eyes met before he had reached where she was standing and he seemed to pause. His was not a casual glance. She felt, in its white hot intensity, as if she had been stripped bare, exposed for the fraud she was. *Could he know*, she wondered, her heart skipping a beat? Wilfred and Minnie had assured her that no one here could, but his expression seemed to say otherwise.

In the next moment, his glance became the casual look one gave a stranger at a party. But something inside her had lifted. A door had opened upon a room she had not even realized was there. She was not, had not been for several years, a virgin, but nothing she had experienced before now had prepared her for the heat that went through her at this fleeting look from a man she had not even met.

'Miss Hale, may I present my assistant, Mr. Paul Winters?' Dr. Everson said, effecting the introduction in a voice chill with disapproval. 'Our hostess, Miss Isabella Hale.'

'How do you do,' he greeted Carol. His greeting was offhand, even arrogant. Everyone else here had been obsequious and fawning. She did not quite know whether to be amused or annoyed by his brusque manner.

'I hope you had no difficulty finding us,' she said, a pointed reminder that he was late.

'None,' he said. 'I simply got a late start. We have a great deal of work to do at the Foundation, and too few people to do it. I was working on something important.'

'And we're not important?' She had instinctively reacted to his arrogance and his all too obvious disapproval of her.

He lifted a mocking eyebrow. 'Quite the contrary. I consider you very important, Miss Hale, more so than you might imagine.' His half smile explained in just what way he considered her important. 'I'm not very good at the diplomatic side of things. Dr. Everson has those chores to handle.'

'Merciful Heavens,' Minnie exclaimed, clucking her tongue, 'you don't even have a drink yet, young man. Come along with me, I'll fix that in a hurry.'

She took Mr. Winters' arm. He allowed himself to be piloted away, with a brief nod in Carol's direction. Wilfred materialized as if from nowhere, stepping neatly into the conversation with Dr. Everson.

Carol let her glance follow Minnie and Mr. Winters. He was very tall and broad of shoulder. He did not look back. Having once decided where he was going, he went directly to it.

Her face was still burning. She had come out the loser in their little exchange. Far worse was the knowledge that she had deserved it.

'Don't you think so, Miss Hale?'

It was a moment before she realized that Dr. Everson had spoken to her. She turned and found his eyes scanning her face.

'I think you're quite right,' she said, giving the doctor a smile. She saw Wilfred relax a little, too. She was here to do a job, not to get herself worked up over an attractive — and prickly — man.

She chatted with the doctor and Wilfred, maintaining a flow of small talk, but another part of her mind was wondering: if Paul Winters disapproved of her sort of person, and of this sort of money raising, why had he supposedly insisted on being here?

Again her eyes sought him out. He was listening to Minnie, and none too eagerly. He was plainly not of the cocktail party circuit. This was a man who would rather be 'doing' than standing around talking about doing.

Why was he here?

Suddenly he had noticed her gaze and was looking back at her. Once again their eyes met . . . and something crackled between them, leaping across the space between them.

She realized he had come to see her. She did not know for what purpose. The look in his eyes was not respectful, nor admiring, nor even lustful.

He looked at her with pure, raw hatred! As she sensed it, she shivered involuntarily.

'Are you cold?' Wilfred asked.

'No,' she said quickly, 'I was just thinking of something. Something unpleasant.'

'Tut-tut,' Dr. Everson said, 'a pretty little thing like you ought to have nothing but pretty thoughts in her head.'

She laughed and joined in the conversation, but something inside her shivered. Without knowing why, she felt frightened.

★　★　★

'I think,' Wilfred said, 'we can go in to dinner. Isabella, will you escort Dr. Everson?'

'But no,' the doctor seized her arm with enthusiasm, steering Carol toward the door, 'I will escort your lovely niece.'

Carol sat at one end of the table with the doctor at her right. Wilfred was at the opposite end. Minnie had seated herself halfway along the table.

Dinner was the sort one expected at testimonial banquets. The roast beef was cold, the potatoes dry. The service was efficient, however. Watching the seeming army of servants come and go, Carol could not help being impressed herself at how wealthy 'she' was.

Of course most of this help was only temporary. Isabella kept a house in Florida and one in Southern California. From what she gathered, Wilfred and Minnie spent most of their time at one or the other of those places.

The food and the service being what they were, the dinner went quickly. Dr.

Everson had plainly set his mind to charming her. His stream of words seemed to come from some endless source.

Dessert came and went. Coffee was served. Finally, it was time to get to the purpose of the evening.

Wilfred had written a little delivery speech for her and coached her in it. It was short and simple, explaining only that, as the problems of children were a matter of special interest to her, she was making a gift of one million dollars to the World's Children Foundation.

Carol saw Wilfred signal the butler and a moment later he was brought a small silver tray with an envelope on it. He examined the contents of the envelope and finding them apparently to his satisfaction, motioned for the butler to bring the tray to Carol.

Carol studied the check inside the envelope quickly but with a sharp eye. It was made out for an even million dollars to The World's Children Foundation. Wilfred had signed his name to it.

She was satisfied Wilfred had kept his

word. However personally unlikable she might find him, he was not a crook, it seemed. At the very worst, he was a sort of Robin Hood.

Wilfred had stood while she examined the check, attracting the attention of those at the table toward him rather than her, with the exception of his wife. Carol looked up to find Mrs. Hale watching her intently. She smiled when Carol looked at her, and turned with the others toward Wilfred.

'I hope everyone enjoyed their dinner as much as I did,' Wilfred said. Minnie led the polite round of applause that followed. Carol noted that Paul Winters did not applaud at all.

'First,' Wilfred went on, 'I want to welcome all of you to Hale House. I think it is safe to assume that most of us know why we are here.'

Wilfred let the little flurry of laughter die before he went on. He spoke of Isabella Hale's legendary generosity, of the keen interest she had taken over the last several years in the problems of children about the globe. He made her sound altogether noble and heroic.

Carol found herself wondering if Isabella Hale were really like that. 'I am Isabella,' she had told herself over and over, facing herself in the mirror. It was strange that the woman she was impersonating was utterly unknown to her. She knew a few superficial details, of dress and family history, enough to fend off any troublesome questions, but the real Isabella was as shadowy and mysterious to her as if they came from different planets.

The impressions she did have of Isabella were quite contradictory. She had a vague recollection of that 'madcap heiress' description, but that was certainly at odds with the image of the sober-minded philanthropist devoting her time and her resources to helping needy children.

Done on a small scale, those philanthropic efforts might have been only a sham, a matter of maintaining good press, or even trying to establish tax breaks. From Wilfred's remarks, however, it would seem as if Isabella had had no press at all, certainly not in years, and wanted none.

The woman had spent virtually all of her time these past several years in this general line of work, and giving away money.

There was something Wilfred had said, on their first meeting, about some sort of trouble. He had mentioned a scandal, but had he said of what kind? She did not recall, and nothing came from a search of her own memory.

'Well,' Wilfred was saying, 'I think the best thing to do now is just to introduce her and let her talk for herself. Ladies and gentlemen, my niece, Miss Isabella Hale.'

Carol felt prepared for this moment — until she looked down the table at Paul Winters. He was watching her closely, with a look of such venom, it completely unnerved her. She managed to get to her feet, but her well-rehearsed speech went completely out of her head.

There was a current of embarrassed movement along the table. She remembered, finally, and began to speak falteringly. She knew Wilfred and Minnie were in agony. Her face was flushed and the more she commanded herself to act calmly, the more flustered she became.

She cut the already brief speech short. 'I've never cared for the limelight,' she said, and saw Wilfred relax for the first time since she had stood. 'Forgive me, please, for making this so brief. Dr. Everson, I hope you will accept this gift on behalf of The World's Children Foundation.' She thrust the envelope with the check at the doctor, virtually under his nose.

He clearly had not expected her speech to end so soon or so abruptly. He seized the check, crumpling the envelope, and got to his feet.

In that moment, something quite unexpected occurred. Paul Winters got to his feet. Heads turned in his direction. Carol found her eyes locked with his again. She thought at first that he meant to rescue his colleague from his moment of embarrassment.

'While my friend, Dr. Everson, is getting his thoughts together,' Mr. Winters said, in a voice that seemed to fill the room effortlessly, 'I would like to take this opportunity to propose a toast to our hostess.'

The guests lifted their glasses with his.

'To Isabella Hale,' he said. 'Millionairess, world traveler, philanthropist . . . ' he paused a fraction of a second before adding, 'and murderess.'

There was a flutter of movement along the table and several astonished gasps. Carol's hand went to her throat in an instinctive gesture.

'Just a moment, young man,' Wilfred said from his end of the table, but everyone ignored him.

'You've forgotten that we have met before, haven't you?' Paul Winters asked Carol down the table.

'Yes . . . I . . . ' she stammered, looking down the table to Wilfred for help, but he was seemingly too astonished to do anything.

'I've waited six years to see you again.' Winters grinned sardonically at her confusion. 'Six long years of waiting to confront the woman who murdered my brother.'

For a brief space in time it seemed as if they were both of them frozen in place.

Wilfred came to life finally. He went angrily to the door that led to the kitchen and barked some orders. A moment later both Harley, the butler, and the husky young chauffeur appeared.

'Throw that man out of here,' Wilfred ordered, pointing at Paul Winters. 'Toss him out of the house and see that he leaves in his car. We don't want him skulking around later.'

The two men looked pleased with their orders. Paul Winters stepped quickly back from the table, sending his chair crashing over backwards and backed toward the wall, prepared to defend himself. The other guests sat in stupefied silence, some of them looking horrified while others seemed to look forward to a good brawl.

Standing at the end of the table, watching the slow advance of Wilfred's two servants, Carol tried to put some order into her whirling thoughts. A murderess . . . ? A scandal six years before . . . ? 'Six long years of waiting . . . ?' he'd said. What had she gotten herself into with this seemingly innocent deception?

'Stop,' she said aloud, addressing the two servants.

Her command was so unexpected, so sudden in the hush that had fallen over the room, that the men actually did stop.

They, and everyone else present, gaped at her. No one looked more surprised than Wilfred.

'Stay out of this,' Wilfred said after a pause, motioning the men to go on. 'I will handle it.'

'No,' Carol said with as much authority as she could summon. 'I will handle it myself.'

She met Wilfred's angry gaze, tossing the challenge at him boldly. She was calling his bluff, and he was furious.

'Now wait just a minute,' Minnie said, getting hurriedly to her feet.

'This is my house,' Carol said loudly and firmly, 'and I will give the orders here, thank you. I want to talk to Mr. Winters.'

Minnie was on the verge of saying something else. It was no doubt this that decided the matter for Wilfred. He could see the anger in his wife's face. He knew her lack of discretion. She could very well spill the whole thing before she knew what she was saying.

'Very well,' he said aloud, with a sigh of resignation. 'Isabella is right, my dear. It is her house, after all. I personally think

Mr. Winters has been exceedingly rude, and my chivalrous instinct is to defend my niece's honor, but if she feels differently . . . ' He shrugged and motioned Minnie to be quiet. To the two servants, who had been watching the scene keenly, he said, 'You may go, but stay close, in case we need you.'

Carol had been watching Wilfred and Minnie. When she turned her attention back to Paul Winters, she was annoyed to discover that he appeared amused.

'And now,' he said, coming back to the table again, to sip his wine, 'I suppose you're going to give me orders too?'

She nearly said she found it impossible to imagine anyone giving this towering man orders. 'I would like to talk to you, please, she said instead. 'Will you come into the library with me?'

'And if I don't? You'll bring your dressed up thugs back, I suppose.'

She started from the room, pausing at the door to look back and say, 'Please?'

He followed her. She led the way to the library. A fire was burning low in the fireplace there. 'Will you have a drink?'

she asked him. 'I think I could use one myself, frankly.'

His cold manner softened, very slightly, but it gave her some hope that she could lessen his hatred.

He went to the tray and examined the bottles. 'Cognac?' he asked, lifting one of the bottles. She nodded and he poured a brandy for each of them.

She fully realized she was playing a dangerous game. At any minute she could trip herself up and reveal herself as an imposter. He knew something, however, that she did not know and that, she realized now, she should have learned before this — the nature of the scandal in Isabella's past.

Her seemingly innocent deception in impersonating Isabella suddenly seemed ominous and frightening. She might be into something far more serious than she had imagined. She had to learn the truth.

Their fingers touched lightly as he gave her the glass. No good trying to deceive herself. She did not want this man to hate her, even if it was really someone else he hated. For a fleeting instant she was tempted to begin by telling him the truth of who she was.

She could not do that, of course. It was not she alone who was involved in this charade. She had a commitment with Wilfred and Minnie, and so long as there was no evidence of wrongdoing on their part, it would be dishonorable of her to betray their confidence.

It almost seemed as if he sensed some of this struggle within her. She perceived a momentary softening in his attitude.

She walked toward the French doors and took a deep breath, willing her heart to resume its normal pace.

'I wanted you to explain things to me,' she said. 'You said I had met you before. Tell me where.'

He looked bewildered.

'Doesn't my name mean anything to you? I expected you to react when we were introduced. My God, I thought you were cool. It was a shock when I finally realized you didn't even know who I was.'

'I thought . . . ' She paused and turned to face him. 'But, I'm not at all sure. Please, tell me why you hate me as you do.'

He studied her face for a moment, looking genuinely puzzled. 'We met at a hearing, in a courtroom,' he said, watching her intently. 'At least, we were never introduced, but we saw one another. I knew who you were, certainly, and you knew who I was.'

A little tremor of relief went through her. They had not actually met, he and Isabella. So he might not recognize her for the fraud she was. He had *seen* Isabella — quite a different thing — at a legal hearing of some sort. Perhaps at a distance. Certainly at a time that had apparently been charged emotionally for him, so that his memory might not be clear at all. A girl of sixteen and a woman of twenty-two could be entirely different creatures.

He was still waiting for her to remember the scene. How could she tell him that she would never remember it, because she had not been there?

'Go on,' she prodded him gently.

He set his glass angrily aside and, before she could step back from him, he seized her by the shoulders, his fingers cutting into the soft flesh there.

'Don't you even remember?' he demanded. 'Did what happened then mean so very little to you?'

She swallowed. Her entire body was shaking in his grip, and not entirely from fear.

'You know what I was like before . . . before that happened.' She said. 'And you certainly know what I've been like since. Can't you see how it changed me, changed my life?'

It was a straw she had clutched at, and yet she felt that what she was saying was true. Without knowing Isabella, or even what had happened, she could see that her life had been altered drastically. Surely that was a result of what had occurred at that fateful time in the past, whatever that had been.

Her desperate stab worked. He let go of her. Her skin burned where he had clutched her.

'Yes, of course, you're right,' he said. His shoulders drooped. He took up his glass again and drained it in one long draught.

'I've seen all that for myself,' he said. 'All of the work with children. Your donations, even the donation to the World's Children Foundation. I thought maybe they were a sham, or a way of wiping out your guilt. I thought that a person as cold and selfish as you could never change. And yet, when I look at you, I see another person entirely from the one I saw six years ago.'

Her heart skipped a beat. This was too close to the truth. 'Perhaps I am another person,' she said.

'Yes.' He came to stand so close to her that she could feel his breath on her forehead when she looked up at him. 'Who are you?' he asked in a whisper.

She wanted desperately to tell him the truth, but she could not. 'I am Isabella. Isabella Hale.'

Again he searched her face, her eyes, seeming to probe the very depths of her soul. The silence grew so lengthy, she asked, 'What do you see?'

'Something that completely astonishes me. I see a woman who is very gentle, shy even. One who cares about people and about life. A woman with a vast and, I think, untapped reservoir of love.'

Her temples were pounding. She dared not trust her voice.

'I came here hating you,' he went on. 'I've hated you for six years. Until now, I think a part of me wanted to kill you.'

It seemed almost as if it was another woman, another voice and not hers that asked, 'And now?'

'And now . . . ' Then, so suddenly that she had no time to anticipate it, he had seized her in his arms and his mouth was upon hers.

The room seemed to spin around. It was like stepping from one dimension into another one, an entirely different world from the one in which she had lived before, and she knew the old pallid world would never be the same for her again.

One minute she was in his arms. The next she was standing dazed and trembling and he was gone. The door behind her crashed open and he went out, in that swift, determined way he had, leaving her behind, alone.

3

It seemed an eternity ago that she had left the guests in the dining room, but in reality it was less than five minutes. They'd barely had time to retire once more to the drawing room, where they were having after dinner drinks, when Carol rejoined them.

All eyes were upon her as she came in. It was only natural that everyone was curious, and her dazed appearance could only have added to their curiosity.

She went directly to Wilfred. He met her in the center of the room, clearly both annoyed and anxious, but also as curious as the others. Minnie, who had been in the middle of an animated conversation with one of the guests, stared at her, open-mouthed and resentful.

'I want to talk to you,' Carol greeted Wilfred.

He smiled and replied in a low tone, 'Perhaps it could wait until later, after our guests have retired.'

His voice was pitched so that it would not carry. 'I'd like to talk to you now,' she said, loudly and clearly.

He had only two alternatives — to create a scene, or to acquiesce.

'Of course, if you insist.' He bowed slightly and with a wave of his hand motioned for her to lead the way.

In the hall, however, his manner became decidedly less servile. 'In here,' he said shortly, indicating a door.

She followed him into the room and turned to face him as he closed and locked the door behind them. He was obviously angry, but his anger did not in the least intimidate her. She too was angry. Something important had been hidden from her and she meant to know what it was before this deception went any further.

'How dare you?' Wilfred demanded. 'Where do you get off ordering me about? Have you forgotten who I am? And who you are?'

'I am Isabella Hale. Or have you forgotten? You made me into Isabella

Hale, if only for tonight. And so long as I am here and expected to impersonate your niece, you will treat me as if I were her.'

His lips tightened. 'And if I don't?'

'Then I will blow your entire scheme sky-high. I'll walk back into that drawing room right now and tell all of those people exactly who I am and how I happened to be here.'

'I can stop you from doing that.'

'By calling for your thugs? I warn you, if anyone lays a hand on me I will start screaming like a banshee. There's an entire roomful of people just next door who would certainly find that astonishing. I think one or two of them would come to investigate.'

Abruptly he relaxed slightly, his manner becoming less ferocious.

'I think we're both letting our tempers get the better of us.' He took his time lighting a cigarette.

'Where is Mr. Winters?' he asked through a cloud of smoke.

'If I am any judge, he's in his room packing to leave. Don't look so pleased. I don't want him to go.'

'You can't mean that,' he said, astonished.

'But I do. I want him to stay on a little longer.'

'Don't be a fool. The sooner he goes, the better. Besides, even if he were to stay the night, he would still have to leave in the morning with the other guests.'

She changed tack. 'What was he talking about at the dinner table? What happened six years ago to your niece?'

Wilfred's eyes narrowed. 'Didn't he tell you about it?'

'No. Not all of it, at least.'

'It's nothing that concerns you, frankly. It has nothing to do with any of what's happened tonight.'

'I don't believe that,' she said impatiently. 'I have a right to know. I don't like being mixed up in murder, or anything close to it. If you won't tell me about it, I shall . . .'

'Go to the police?' he suggested. For the first time since they had come into the room, he looked amused. 'I assure you the police looked into this so-called murder long ago, and satisfied themselves completely.'

'Then perhaps you will be so good as to satisfy me.'

He sighed and puffed on his cigarette, looking less annoyed now than bored. But she had the suspicion that he was acting.

'My niece was quite young when her parents died,' he said, apparently giving in. 'Their wills made me the trustee of their estates. I was given the authority, with certain limitations, to handle her money and her, until she was of age.

'The first part was simple. I had always been a financial advisor to my brother, so handling her money was not much more than a continuation of what I had been doing. The second part, handling her, was not so easy, though. If you had kept a closer eye on the newspaper reports of that period, you would know that Isabella Hale was a willful, headstrong girl. She was a spoiled brat. It was fortunate indeed that I held the purse strings. If she'd had her way, she'd have gone through her entire fortune in no time at all. Nearly every week it was some new idea, some harebrained scheme, some worthless friend who wanted her to invest in some worthless plan, or some man she had a crush on and wanted to shower with gifts. She had no sense of judgment. How could she? She'd never had to think for herself.

'I kept control of the money and turned a deaf ear to her schemes, for which she was able to thank me later. Yes, I assure you, she did come to thank me. But when she was in her teens, we had more than a few sharp words.'

He paused again, seeming to remember what it had been like. Listening to him, Carol felt oddly uneasy. She was getting the impression he had never been fond of Isabella. She wondered if Wilfred had been the poor relation.

'But while I controlled the money, when it came to her personal life, she ran free. She cared nothing for anybody's opinion. Cared nothing for anybody, period, beyond the most superficial level.

'But, no that isn't quite right either, because she often seemed actively intent on hurting people. If she drove a car too fast, or badgered her friends into taking reckless chances, or created a general disturbance, you had a feeling that she was actually hoping for the worst to happen.

'Of course, eventually the worst possible thing did happen. Not too surprisingly, when it did, it was not to her or her wild-living friends that it happened, but to someone quite innocent.

'She had been out partying with a group of her friends. They were a wild group, drinking, doping, carousing, keeping all hours.'

Again there was that unmistakable note of disdain in his voice. Perhaps Wilfred had secretly wanted to be a part of that libertine group, despite his disapproval of them.

'They were in two separate cars, going from one party to another at Isabella's apartment. Isabella was driving one of the cars, and she turned a simple drive home into a high-speed race. This was not in the open country, mind you, it was in the city. It was late. There were few cars on the streets where they were. I have no doubt that to them it made some kind of cockeyed sense to have their lights off, so the police would be less likely to see them. As I said, they were certainly drunk, probably stoned, too.'

He smiled reflectively at his memories, not a pleasant smile. 'Paul Winters. Yes, I should have remembered the name. Of course, I only saw him once, briefly, across a courtroom. Mr. Winters was not here, in the states when the accident occurred. He was in the Marine Corps, as I recall. He got back to this country for the last of the hearings, long after the accident had occurred.

'The night of the accident, his younger brother was out. I think he and his mother had been visiting some relative at the shore. They were returning late. The boy — if I remember rightly, he would have been six, maybe seven years old at the time — he was running ahead of his mother. Isabella was driving at high speed, with her lights off. Neither of them must have seen the other until it was too late.'

Carol gasped, covering her face with

her hands, the picture Wilfred had sketched for her altogether too vivid in her mind.

'How awful,' she said. 'It was . . . it really was murder, just like he said.'

'In a sense, you might say so.' Wilfred seemed to consider it less horrible than she did. 'An attorney would call it manslaughter. Or, alleged manslaughter, until it was a proven thing.'

It was a second or two before she grasped the significance of his remarks. 'It was never proven?'

'Isabella was a very wealthy woman, and my niece. I had a duty to protect and help her in any way I could. The testimony in court presented the entire incident in a different light.'

'But how could it? Facts are facts.'

'Facts are often subject to interpretation. There was simply no evidence to prove any real guilt on Isabella's part. The mother testified that the car was coming fast, but there was no way of establishing how fast. The second car, with Isabella's friends in it, never came into the picture at all. They hightailed it when the accident occurred. No one outside of our family and the attorneys knew of the existence of another car full of people.'

'But Isabella was driving without lights, that much the mother must have seen.'

'How do you know that? You only say that because I told you so. The mother did say that the car had been without lights, but Isabella insisted they were on. And there was a witness who eventually came forward, who testified that Isabella's car had passed her several blocks back, and that the lights had been on then. It made no sense to suppose Isabella had simply switched them off afterwards. Who would drive the streets at night with their lights off, after all? When all was said and done, it seemed most likely that the boy, in a gay mood, tired and careless, had simply run into the path of an oncoming car.'

'But Isabella knew better, if no one else did. If she had only told the truth, things would have turned out differently. The real tragedy was that she did not accept responsibility for her actions.'

'And had she done so, the outcome

would still have been tragic — for her. She was a young woman, hardly more than a child. To be convicted of those charges could have ruined her life. Moreover, I had a sworn duty to protect my niece's interests. I simply could not permit her to testify against herself. The law doesn't require that either.'

So, Paul Winters had been right. Isabella really was a murderess, who had evaded justice by virtue of her wealth. This was the woman she had agreed to impersonate.

The woman Paul Winters believed her to be. Little wonder that he hated her the way he did.

'As you can see,' Wilfred concluded, 'however melodramatic Mr. Winters might have made his charges sound, there is no murder lurking in the shadows that you need concern yourself with. You are involved in no scheme more nefarious than what I have already told you of, that of making a generous donation to a worthy charity. I trust this puts your mind somewhat at ease.'

'A little,' she said. 'Nonetheless, I

would like to ask Mr. Winters to stay on a bit longer than the other guests. An additional day, perhaps.'

'But why?'

'He did see Isabella Hale, even if it was only that one time in the courtroom. I think he harbors suspicions that I am not who I am supposed to be. And I think if I can have a little time with him, I might be able to allay his suspicions. Don't you agree that it would be best if I could do so?'

It was not the truth. Even had she been able to explain her true motives for wanting Paul to stay, Wilfred would at best have laughed at her.

She knew that she wanted to relieve some of the bitterness that still festered within him, if only for his own sake. She felt too that she wanted to offer him a case for the other side — for Isabella, if not for herself.

Perhaps in the long run what she really wanted was to win his approval, regardless of who he believed her to be.

Luckily Wilfred did not question her motives further. 'Maybe you are right,' he said. 'It might be best to invite him to stay an extra night, so we can assure ourselves that he suspects nothing.'

She could not see that it would greatly matter if, by that time, Winters did suspect that she was not the real Isabella Hale. The dinner would have been long ended, the presentation made, the other guests gone. At the worst he might have gone to the newspapers with a far-fetched story that, even if someone should believe him, would not make for very exciting news.

However, Wilfred's desires coincided this once with hers. 'I'll ask him myself,' she said. 'Right now, before he has a chance to leave.'

'Don't you think we ought to be with our guests? This entire business has surely seemed a bit peculiar to them.'

'Is it really necessary that I be there, though? Wouldn't they expect me to be shaken up over the scene Mr. Winters created?'

Wilfred smiled, apparently pleased by this change in her manner toward him. 'Why don't we compromise? How about if you make an appearance, just long enough to explain that to them yourself, and tender your apologies, after which you can retire, and I will see to the rest of it.'

She thought it best to agree. Wilfred was really rather easy to manage. So long as he was made to feel important and wise, everything was all right.

The guests accepted her apologies graciously, although several of looked as if they would have liked to have their curiosity sated a little further.

'I'm afraid I have a bit of a headache,' she explained, standing in the doorway to the drawing room. 'The long trip down, and then that dreadful scene. Please make yourselves at home. My uncle and aunt will see that everything is taken care of, and I will see you all before you leave in the morning. Good night.'

To a chorus of goodnights, she left them and went up the stairs. Wilfred had already told her which room was Paul Winters'. He looked surprised to see her. She could see that he had been packing to go.

'Miss Hale,' he said, recovering quickly from the surprise of finding her at his door. 'I'm afraid I have behaved pretty badly. I want to apologize, and assure you that you needn't fear any further embarrassment on my behalf. As you can see for yourself, I'll be leaving in the next half hour or so.'

'Mr. Winters . . . ' She hesitated. 'May I come in?'

He stepped to one side. 'It is your house, after all.'

She came in, closing the door. She was suddenly aware of being alone with him, in a bedroom.

'I feel that it is I who owe you an apology, Mr. Winters. The difficulty is, mine can't be expressed with a few words, or in a moment or two. I have come to ask you to stay on for a day, so that we can have an opportunity to talk together.'

He stiffened visibly. She could feel his resistance like a wall between them. 'I don't think that's at all necessary,' he said. 'I've offered my apologies, now I accept yours. Let's let the past be the past and forget it all, shall we?'

'Can we?' she challenged him. 'You said you've carried this bitterness within you for six long years. I can assure you that Isabella Hale has suffered too. We can't erase all of that with a simple, 'I'm sorry'.'

He took a moment to consider what she had said. 'I'm not so sure,' he said.

'Please stay for one more day. I think it might be important to your happiness, and I know it is important to mine.'

He stood looking down at her in that hard way of his. When he spoke, his words were not at all what she had expected.

'There's something about you — something that's downright frightening,' he said. 'I can understand men rushing to do your bidding, to look after you. You bring that out in a man, the urge to take care of you, to protect you.'

'Stay, please,' she said in a small, tight voice. 'One more day. I promise I won't ask more than that.'

'It can't matter much, I suppose.' To her delight, he smiled briefly. 'I have a feeling I'm out of a job anyway, after tonight. Dr. Everson doesn't like being upstaged.'

'Then I shall have that on my conscience as well. And I'm afraid it's been much burdened as it is. You will stay?'

He grew sober again. 'Yes.'

'I'm glad to hear it. I'll leave you then.' In the hall, she paused to look back and say, 'Good night.'

There was nothing timid about the way he was watching her. Whatever he thought of her as a person, Paul Winters found her desirable as a woman. She half expected him to come after her, to bring her back into the room.

But he only said, 'Good night,' and closed the door softly.

* * *

It was not until much later, when they were alone in their bedroom, that Wilfred was able to fill his wife in on his conversation with Carol.

'That girl is too foxy,' Minnie said when she'd heard the entire story. 'I smell a rat.'

'There's nothing to worry about.' He

would have liked nothing more than to be rid of his wife, but of course he could never hope for a divorce now, with what they were into together. This scheme had been hers initially, but from the moment he had agreed to it, he had sealed his fate. Still, if he could not get free of her, he thought himself capable of managing her.

'It's only for another day. Miss Andrews rather naively thinks I gave in to her wishes. She seems to have some sort of crush on Mr. Winters.'

'He is a certainly a good looking hunk of man,' Minnie said, in that crass way of hers that grated on his nerves. 'If I was a few years younger I'd give her a run for her money.'

'I just want to be sure he does not really suspect anything. She suggested that he did. Frankly, I consider that pretty unlikely but we cannot afford to take the slightest chance. The consequences are too dire to contemplate. Having him stay a bit longer gives me the opportunity to sound him out as well. If everything seems all right, I'll send him on his way morning after tomorrow.'

Minnie's eyes shifted. 'You said she's got a crush on him. What if she decides to leave with Winters when he goes?'

He smiled. 'She will not be leaving here,' he promised. He did not add, ' . . . with Mr. Winters.'

4

Carol woke in the morning with a feeling of excitement that brought her from her bed humming. In the bathroom, scrubbing her teeth, she caught sight of her reflection in the mirror over the sink. She looked flushed and eager. Careful, she warned herself.

Wilfred had arranged for her breakfast to be served in her room. The guests were breakfasting downstairs, buffet style, before they departed. She would have liked to be with them — or at least with one person in particular.

She was still in Wilfred's employ, however, and she did as he had arranged, eating more hurriedly than was her custom.

She had dressed in a beige linen suite with a green silk scarf at her throat that picked up the color of her eyes. She looked young and fresh and very pretty as she came down to bid her guests farewell.

The downstairs hall was filled with people. She was aware of the many eyes that turned to watch her descend the stairs, but her own eyes sought and found the one person she wanted to see.

He might have been alone, so aloof did he seem from the people about him. He too turned as she started down and when he saw her, his lips turned in that strange smile of his that set her heart pounding.

Their greeting was nothing more than a brief 'Good morning.' She had other guests to whom she must give her attention for the moment. Wilfred and Minnie were there too, saying lengthy goodbyes to some of the people.

Dr. Everson, as the highest ranking guest, made a lengthy goodbye speech to her. When he had finished it, he said, in the manner of an aside, 'I must apologize again for that unpleasant incident last night. I can assure you that the young man is no longer in our employ.'

She could not resist murmuring, 'That is unfortunate.' The doctor looked quite bewildered, but she did not give him the opportunity to pursue the matter further.

The last of the guests were gone finally, and only Paul Winters remained. At Wilfred's suggestion, he had retired to Wilfred's study while the others departed.

Carol found him there reading a book, but he put it aside and stood as she came into the room.

'Forgive me for taking so long,' she said, a little breathless. 'All those people . . . '

He gave her a nod. 'I quite understand.'

Despite her excitement in being with him, she was not unaware of the risks she was running. Her every instinct told her that Paul Winters was not a man to be trifled with, and she knew she was on thin ice by keeping him close at hand. She would need all of her wits and intelligence if she wanted to prevent him from suspecting that she was not the person she pretended to be.

Did it matter if he discovered the truth? The question came unbidden to her mind, and at once she answered it, yes. In accepting the job, she had given Wilfred her promise to carry the impersonation through to its conclusion. For the truth to

74

come out now would be embarrassing for Wilfred and Minnie, and most of all for the real Isabella. She had made a commitment and it was important now to stick to it.

'Are you enjoying Hale House?' she asked, a little shyly.

'It's certainly very nice. I was hoping maybe you would show me around the grounds — if you have the time.'

'Of course.' She had studied drawings and plans and, without having had more than a glimpse or two of the grounds, she was confident she knew her way around them. 'We can go out this way,' she added, indicating the doors to the flagstone terrace outside.

The terrace, beginning at the front of the house, went about the west side of the house, to form a patio to the rear. The swimming pool there was empty now of all but a few dead leaves on the bottom. The gravel drive went around the opposite end of the house, to the garages. They walked along the terrace.

'It is certainly a beautiful setting for a house,' he said, looking out at the view.

'Did you plan it?'

'No, my mother and father lived here, when they weren't in the city. I preferred the city then. Funny how your thinking changes when you grow up. I think I'd like living here now.'

'Then why don't you?'

The question caught her off guard. 'Oh, I've got so much going on, you know. I'm constantly traveling. And it's a long drive to the nearest major airport. You are right, though, it is beautiful.'

There were no houses or buildings for miles to spoil the vista. Hale House was truly isolated from the world around it.

'It's a bit cut off from people,' she said aloud.

'I think I would rather like that.'

She gave him a cautious look. 'Do you really dislike people so much?'

'I like some people.' His replies were so brief that she sensed he did not like to talk about himself. Instead, he kept steering the conversation back to her. She found herself forgetting her fears of him and thinking of him as pleasant company.

They had reached the rear of the

house. Trees had kept some of the view hidden, but here, suddenly, it spread out before them in all its vastness. They could see for miles over the hills, green with the lingering foliage of summer. Below them the road that led to the house twisted its way down the hill.

'How lovely,' she murmured.

'You act as if you had never seen it before.'

She said quickly, 'It's just that it is so new and lovely each time I see it. Tell me,' she said, changing the subject, 'did you grow up in the country? You give that impression.'

'Yes, I did, as a matter of fact. Not here. In Indiana.'

'Tell me about it.'

He looked down at her with that half smile on his face. 'Perhaps some time I shall,' he said. 'But to be honest, I am not one of my own favorite topics for conversation. I would much prefer to talk about you.'

She wondered if his reluctance to talk of himself was because he was unhappy. Obviously he had suffered a great deal of bitterness over the death of his brother.

'I'm glad we had this chance to be alone,' he said.

'Why didn't you just tell me up front who you were?' she asked. 'When you first got here last night? Or even before you came? If I had known . . . '

'You wouldn't have had me here if you had known in advance.'

She smiled. 'No, you're probably right.' Certainly Wilfred would not have had him here, which was more to the point, but she couldn't tell him that.

When he spoke next, his voice hardened. 'If you could only know what I went through all these years,' he said, speaking as much to himself as to her. 'The sense of injustice that weighed so heavily on me. The loss when my brother died, and the anger I felt when I saw how easily you had cheated justice, wormed your way out of any punishment.'

'No, please.' She put a hand gently upon his arm. 'There are all kinds of punishment.'

He shrugged her hand off and strode to the edge of the terrace, his back to her.

He had suddenly shut her away from him completely.

'None of them truly adequate,' he said in a voice dripping with bitterness. 'None of them sufficient to satisfy what I felt for you. I watched you that one day in the courtroom. You were at a distance, surrounded by a ring of hired hands who let no one come near. I thought I was looking upon the face of evil, a woman completely cruel and heartless.'

She could think of no reply to make. Her pulse was throbbing. 'Perhaps I had better go in,' she said softly.

He turned again and crossed the terrace to where she was standing. 'Forgive me,' he said. 'That was unkind of me. And unfair. I know that you have been punished, within your own heart. Perhaps I knew it all along and would not admit it. I've followed your life since then, your devotion to children and their needs. I know there had to be goodness and sweetness in you to cause you to devote your young life to such causes. Then, when I met you last night, and saw you for myself, at close range, it was a shock. I saw gentleness and kindness. I could hardly believe you were Isabella Hale. I thought someone must have made a mistake. But I realized finally that it was I who had made the mistake. I realized that nothing I or the law might do could have produced the changes that tragic incident produced in you. Have you any idea how greatly you have changed?'

She chose her words carefully. 'I know that it is possible to wreak great harm without truly meaning to. You can do so merely by being selfish and thoughtless. And I know too that once a tragedy has occurred, it cannot be undone.'

'Life would be a lot easier if we could just take back our mistakes.'

'True. But one can, in a sense, make up for them, by using that mistake as the point of beginning for a new life, one that is not selfish and thoughtless. I know that one cannot simply pay you in token for your brother's life, but his death was the cause of a new life for me, one of giving instead of always taking, helping instead of hurting. I shall always carry that burden of guilt with me, but I do not mind because it serves to remind me of the debt I owe to life.'

She truly believed that this must be how Isabella felt. It was the only logical explanation for the dramatic change that had taken place in her, and for the way she had lived her life since the accident.

'I believe you.' He had changed again, becoming gentle. 'I admire you for not trying to say that you were innocent, for admitting your guilt. You're honest and straightforward, and brave.'

'Thank you.' She was trembling slightly but not from fear. Rather, it was with relief that he was no longer so angry. She wanted him to like her, of course, but it was a futile desire. After this day they would certainly never see one another again.

'I seem to be talking like a wild man,' he said. 'I came here hating you, and then when I saw you, I thought you were the most beautiful thing in the world. Suddenly all the things I wanted to say to you seemed unreal, and unimportant. I wanted to punish you during that time, to make you cry, make you suffer.

'Now all of that has changed. Are you

some kind of witch, that all you have to do is look at a man with those emerald green eyes of yours and he becomes your slave?'

'No, I think that you simply faced up to the fact that nothing can change the past or alter what has happened. I am not the woman you saw on that day six years ago, but neither are you the same man you were then. This is today and we are who we are.'

She paused, thinking perhaps she had said too much. Her nerves were stretched tight. The strain of pretending was beginning to take its toll on her.

'And now,' she said, 'I really do think I had better go in. Please, make yourself at home. I'll see you at lunch.'

She left him standing by the edge of the terrace and made her way back toward the house. As she neared the corner, womanly curiosity made her look back.

He was staring after her, but this time he was not grinning sardonically at her. There was an entirely different expression on his face, one she had not seen there before and did not quite understand.

She thought as she went up the stairs to her room that she had not acquitted herself badly. She had answered questions and accusations about a time and an incident that were meaningless to her. Yet the man with her had apparently not suspected that she was not who she seemed to be.

She felt as if she had fought a dangerous battle and come out of it victorious.

At the very least, she had drained some of the unhappiness from within him. She had defended a woman she had never met but whom she knew to be generous and charitable. Perhaps most important of all, she had braved the fears of her own heart.

She spent the rest of the morning in her room. When she came down for lunch, she found Mr. Winters already seated at the table with Wilfred and Minnie. Wilfred and Paul were engaged in a discussion of the stock market.

'Ah, how lovely you look, my dear,' Wilfred greeted her warmly. Mr. Winters' greeting was only a nod, but the look he gave her was approving.

The conversation at lunch was of a general nature, but Minnie and Wilfred questioned Mr. Winters about his interests and his background. Carol observed silently that he managed to make polite replies to their questions while at the same time actually saying almost nothing about himself.

She herself took little part in the conversation except to make polite replies when something was directed at her. Several times she caught Mr. Winters looking across the table at her in a manner that might have been conspiratorial, as if they shared a secret between them.

'And now,' Wilfred said when lunch was finished, 'I hope, Mr. Winters, that you will honor me with a game of billiards. Dr. Everson informed me early on that you played, and I have been looking forward to it since I heard you were staying over. Neither Minnie nor Isabella plays, you see.'

Mr. Winters agreed with no more than the slightest hesitation and the two men retired to the billiard room. Minnie announced that she was going up to her room to rest and Carol was left to herself. The house was quiet now that the servants had gone, except for the housekeeper, Mrs. Green, and the butler, and Carol thought the chauffeur was about somewhere as well.

She decided that some music would be pleasant but she had not seen a stereo or even a radio since she had arrived. Thinking that there must be one somewhere in the house, she went toward the kitchen, in search of Mrs. Green.

The stocky housekeeper was working in the kitchen. She looked at Carol coldly and did not answer Carol's friendly greeting

Undeterred, Carol said, 'I was wondering if there is a radio somewhere in the house that I might put in my room.'

'I expect there is,' Mrs. Green replied curtly. She had been loading the dishes from lunch into a dishwasher, and she went back to her work.

Not one to be put off so easily, Carol asked, 'Can you tell me where I might find one?'

Mrs. Green slammed a bowl down on

the kitchen counter with such violence that Carol was surprised it didn't shatter, and turned toward her with a show of vehemence that was unexpected and unnerving.

'Look,' she snapped, eyes flashing, 'I have my orders, and I've stuck by them. They told me that when there was others around I was to treat you as if you was Miss Isabella. But you ain't and we both know it, and there's nobody else here at this moment but the two of us, so don't expect me to wait on you when I am busy. Which I am, in case you hadn't noticed.'

With that she once more turned her back on Carol. Face burning, Carol left the room. She was so angry she nearly went directly to Wilfred to tell him what had happened.

Of course, she could not do that. Mr. Winters was with him at the moment. She bit her tongue and made her way upstairs. By the time she reached her room, her anger had subsided a little. Mrs. Green had no doubt been overworked the last few days, with a large dinner party to think of and a houseful of guests.

Anyway, what did the rude woman's bad temper really matter to her? By tomorrow she would be gone from Hale House, and she would surely never see the housekeeper again.

She dismissed that brief scene from her mind and decided to take advantage of the free afternoon to do her hair. She wanted to look her best at dinner, the last time she would see Paul Winters.

When she came down again in the afternoon, she was surprised to find him alone in the library.

'Wilfred went up to his room after our game,' he explained when she asked. 'He said he wanted to rest before dinner.'

'I hope you've enjoyed your day,' Carol said.

'I have indeed. It's been quite different from what I anticipated.'

'And what did you expect?'

He thought for a moment. 'What I really should have said, is that you are different. I don't actually know now what I had in mind. I thought about what I would say to you last night when the opportunity presented itself, to accuse you, so to speak. Oddly I never questioned what would happen after I had done so. I supposed I would be thrown out and that would be that. Which is very nearly what did happen, until you intervened. I certainly never dreamed you would invite me to stay on here after I had insulted you so rudely.'

He paused and then said, 'Can you just erase from your mind all the things I said last night?'

'I'll try. I understand how you must have felt.'

'Nevertheless, I had no right to behave as I did. I've lived with hatred and resentment for so long that I can hardly believe now that they're gone.'

'And are they gone?'

'Yes. It was because when I looked at you after I'd said my piece, I suddenly realized that the things I had said could not be true. No person could look as you do, and be anything but good.'

She realized she was back on thin ice again. 'I — I'm not sure we ought to talk like this,' she stammered.

'I only know that whatever crime

occurred in the past, it is no part of you now. I look into your eyes and it isn't there.'

She was suddenly ashamed of the deception she was practicing with him, when he was baring his innermost thoughts to her. She felt despicable.

He reached out and took her hand. 'You don't have to say anything,' he said gently. 'I can see in your eyes that I too am forgiven. They say the eyes are the window of the soul. What I see in yours makes me ashamed.'

She tried to take her hand from his. 'Please,' she said in a hoarse voice.

'Why do you fight me so?' His voice dropped to little more than a whisper. 'You must know the effect you have on men. Do you think I should be different?'

She knew she should stop him before this conversation went too far, but the words he was saying were like music to her ears.

'When I came into this room last night,' he said, still whispering, 'I had always thought of you as a devil, but you looked like an angel. I told myself it must only be a façade you assumed for the world to see, to keep people from knowing what you really are. But later, when I had spoken to you, and this morning, I realized the truth. I know, now.'

She felt a shiver of alarm. 'You know what?'

'I know you are exactly what you appear to be.'

His words made her feel cheap and dishonest!

She turned her face away. 'You mustn't speak to me like this.'

'Why not? The poison has gone, and something else has taken its place.'

'We don't know one another at all,' she said.

'I know everything I need to know. We only have tonight. Tomorrow we will go our separate ways, unless . . . ' He left that statement unfinished.

She knew what he meant to imply. Unless they stayed together. Not here, of course, she could hardly stay on at Hale House, but if she came to New York with him . . . That suggestion was plain to read in his eyes, in the way his hand clasped hers. It was an invitation she couldn't fail to grasp.

Her head was swimming. This was insane, they had only met — and yet, she felt as if she had known him all her life.

'I think I should go up and dress for dinner,' she managed to say.

'And after dinner?'

'I . . . ' She hesitated.

'I won't let you go until you promise we will be together after dinner.'

'I promise,' she said faintly.

He kissed her, briefly. She did not dare look at him again, but turned and almost ran from the room.

* * *

'There's nothing for us to worry about,' Wilfred was telling Minnie at just that moment. 'He suspects nothing. He's simply gone daft over the girl.'

'Couldn't that be awful dangerous?' Minnie asked. 'If they keep meeting and talking . . . she could let something slip. He's no fool, that one . . . '

Wilfred shrugged, unconcerned. 'There won't be time for anything serious to develop. Mr. Winters is leaving tomorrow morning and that will be the end of it.'

'What about her?'

'She won't cause any trouble. I will see to that.'

5

For dinner she wore a gown of white, and the only piece of 'good' jewelry she herself owned, a choker of golden strands imbedded with pearls. Her hair was piled atop her head, falling down on either side of her face in loose ringlets.

She knew Paul thought she looked enchanting, the truth was plain in his eyes when he gazed at her across the table.

What would he think of her when he learned of her deception? And the longer she continued the deception, the more distasteful it would seem to him later — if there was a later.

She wanted to tell him the truth at the earliest opportunity, but she couldn't do that without consulting Wilfred. She had already considered doing that, but some instinct that she couldn't explain to herself had caused her to put that off.

Something in Wilfred's manner — Minnie's, too — had changed subtly, though she couldn't say exactly what. She had the oddest sensation that Wilfred and Minnie were playacting with her too.

She could not forget that all the things Paul said to her, the way he looked at her, the feel of his strong hands when he took hold of her — these were not hers alone. They belonged to Isabella Hale as well.

It was Carol Andrews he had seen and talked to, but not Carol Andrews as herself. He had seen her playing the role of Isabella.

The things she had said in Isabella's defense, while of course they were things she believed as well, were the things she thought Isabella would have wanted to say.

She felt a wave of disappointment when, after they had finished eating, Wilfred said, 'Would you care for another game of billiards, Mr. Winters?'

'Thank you,' Paul said, 'but Miss Hale has promised to show me the view by moonlight.'

Carol blushed and ignored the mocking look Wilfred gave her — and did not see Minnie's scowl.

The night air was cool. 'Do you want a

wrap?' Paul asked when they were alone outside.

She shook her head. What did she care for such mundane considerations as warm and cold?

He stood looking down at her, his eyes drinking her in. 'White suits you. And it's perfect for a bride.'

'But I'm not a bride,' she said, without thinking. She looked up, to meet his eyes. They were dark, with a glint in them as of a distant fire.

Suddenly she understood, and felt her cheeks turn red. He took her hand in his. 'Do you want me to put it more bluntly?' he asked. 'Very well, then, I will: I love you.'

Her silence did not deter him in the least. 'I think maybe I fell in love with you that first time I saw you, six years ago.'

'We shouldn't talk like this. I should go in.'

Yet she could not go. She wanted to hear him, even if his words hurt her. He reached out to take her in his arms, and she came to him as one in a dream. Their lips met.

The sound of footsteps intruded. Startled, they parted and both looked in that direction. The chauffeur came around the corner of the building. He stopped, seeing them, and stared at them in surprise and puzzlement.

'Excuse me,' he said after a moment, and retraced his steps, disappearing again around the corner. *Going to tell Wilfred and Minnie?* Carol wondered.

'We should go in,' she said.

He took her hand. 'Come to New York with me tomorrow. Let me teach you to love me in return.'

'Please, let's not think of that,' she begged in a whisper.

'Are you made of ice? Doesn't anything I say warm you? Isn't there any fire in you?'

She dared not tell him of the fire was burning within her at this very moment. 'How can you expect a woman to understand you?' she said instead. 'One moment you hate me, the next moment you love me . . . '

'I thought I explained all that.' More gently, he said, 'You've lived with me for years, in my imagination.'

'Maybe you don't know me at all. Maybe you know some other woman.'

He drew her close. She had a moment of fear, when she fluttered in his arms as if she had been captured in flight, but there was no escape. His lips again found hers, holding her helpless, taking her a prisoner.

'I want you,' he whispered. 'And I'll have you. Tonight you will be mine. Tonight and forever.'

It was not her he was making love to, it was Isabella. The response of her body to his was the response of another woman. She was only a pretender, a liar, whom he would despise if he knew the truth. She had no right to listen to him, to feel what she was feeling.

'No,' she cried suddenly, tearing herself from his arms. She stumbled away from him, and began to cry. 'Please.' Her voice broke in a sob. She turned and fled from him, from the terrace. She ran as if demons pursued her, up to her room, locking the door before throwing herself on the bed.

'It wasn't you he was kissing, you fool,' she told herself, and felt a pain like the stab of a knife.

A knock on the door gave her a start. Trembling with anticipation, she went to it and opened it, to find Paul standing there.

'Don't be frightened,' he said, standing well back from the door. 'I won't try to come in or force myself upon you. I've only come to once again apologize.'

'It is I who should apologize.'

He dismissed that with a sweep of his hand. 'I wasn't entirely out of my mind, though,' he went on. 'I do want you to come with me tomorrow. I won't ask that you love me in return, but I want you with me. Will you come?'

It took all of her self-control to say, 'I can't.'

'In that case, I shall say good night.' He gave a little bow and turned from her, and was gone.

She closed her door and began to cry again.

* * *

She woke tired and listless. She had slept haunted by the knowledge that she would part with Paul this day, and forever.

Wilfred and Minnie were in the breakfast room. They greeted her perfunctorily. Carol had coffee and toast and made a few polite attempts at conversation.

After picking at her breakfast, she pushed her plate aside.

Wilfred knew the reason for her lack of appetite and was relieved that it would be leaving Hale House this morning. Before things went any further.

Paul came in a few minutes later, pausing in the doorway. At sight of him, Carol's hand shook so that she spilled some of her coffee.

'Good morning, Mr. Winters,' Minnie greeted him.

'Good morning, Mrs. Hale, Mr. Hale.' His greetings were barely polite. 'I'd like to talk to you before I go, if I may,' he said directly to Carol.

She rose and went wordlessly before him into the hall, ignoring the frosty look she got from Minnie.

'I suppose you're all ready to go,' she said, when they were in the drawing room,

'Almost. But I still want you to come with me.'

'We've discussed this before,' she said. 'It's pointless to go over and over the same issues.'

'Yes. You know how I feel. But there's something more, I don't know exactly what, but it's like a sixth sense telling me that you should not stay here.'

'I can't think of any reason why I should not stay. Wilfred and Minnie are family, after all.'

He looked at her shrewdly. 'Call it a hunch, if you will, but I don't think it's wise for you to stay on here. I think you should come with me. Now.'

'No. I can't. I just can't.'

'What about later, then?' he asked. 'Will you join me later?'

'Perhaps.' Tears were stinging her eyes. 'I will try.'

'All right, I don't understand, but it will be as you wish it. For now, at least. But I won't wait forever. If need be, I'll come back here for you and nothing will stop me then from taking you with me. Is that clear?'

She smiled despite herself at the force of his determination. 'Yes,' she said.

He took her in his arms and kissed her. The kiss was brief, as if neither of them wanted to prolong the agony of parting.

She started to say goodbye but he put a finger gently to her lips. 'No, don't say it,' he whispered. 'Pretend that we are still together, and we will be.'

She was dimly aware that someone had rung the bell at the front door, but there was no need for her to deal with it. Isabella would hardly answer her own front door.

'You had better go now,' she told Paul.

Voices from outside, in the hall, intruded loudly. Wilfred's voice, saying something that could not quite be distinguished, and then another voice, a man's voice that Carol did not recognize.

'I insist upon seeing Isabella,' the strange voice said, and in reply to something said by Wilfred, 'I am Michael Forrest, her fiancé.'

' . . . I'm afraid it's impossible,' Wilfred said.

'Damn you, it's not impossible,' Michael Forrest replied, almost shouting now. 'Is she in there? Is that why you're blocking that door? Get out of my way.'

Carol ran to where Paul was standing and clutched at his arm. She had scarcely reached his side when the door from the hallway crashed open.

A stranger stood framed in the open doorway, with an alarmed Wilfred just behind him. The stranger looked at Paul and then at Carol. 'I want to see Isabella Hale,' he said. 'I'm not leaving until I do. Where the devil is she?'

The intruder was young and under ordinary circumstances he might have been reasonably good-looking. His hair was reddish and worn rather long. He wore glasses, behind which his flashing brown eyes were even more prominent. He was thin, but wiry looking. At the moment he looked as if he were ready for a fight.

'I know Isabella is here and I am not leaving this house until I see her.'

Wilfred followed Michael Forrest into the drawing room, putting a placating hand upon one thin shoulder.

'I promise you that you shall have your wish, if you will only calm yourself down for a moment.'

The doorway was clear, and one quick flick of Wilfred's eyes in that direction told Carol what she must do. 'Please,' she said to Paul and, clinging to his arm, she brought him reluctantly into the hall. He looked back once as if to change his mind and insist upon an explanation, but the door had already closed after them.

Minnie too had been left in the hall. She shot a furtive glance at the closed door, obviously wishing she could be in that room with the two men. Then, flashing a smile at Paul, she said, 'Oh, Mr. Winters. I'm so sorry to see you go. I hope you have enjoyed your stay at Hale House.'

He ignored her. His earlier anger had given way to puzzlement. 'What is all this about?' he asked of Carol. 'Who is that man? And why didn't you . . . ?'

Carol tugged him in the direction of

the front door. 'Please,' she said, 'I don't know him, honestly I don't.'

At the front door, he paused. 'But he said he was your fiancé,' he said.

'Yes.' She thought desperately for some explanation that would satisfy him. 'Wilfred's told me about him. He's what they call a stalker. He seems to have gotten it into his head that he and I are engaged. He's been writing letters and making phone calls. But this is the first time I've ever seen him. Wilfred thought he had managed to get rid of him but it seems not.'

'He didn't act delusional. He seemed genuinely . . . '

'Believe me, this can all be explained in full, but not now, Paul, not here. I'm really concerned for Wilfred.'

He yielded with a final glance in the direction of the closed door to the drawing room.

'You will come to me?'

'Yes.'

'Do you have a cell phone with you?'

The question surprised her. 'Yes, I do. Why?'

'I just wanted to be sure you can call me if anything . . . well, you will call if you need me for any reason, promise?'

'I will, I promise.'

'All right.' He leaned down and kissed her again lightly. 'Till then.'

He got into his car, a nondescript sedan, serviceable without being glamorous. Beside it sat a red sports car, rakish and low-slung, that must belong to Michael Forrest. The convertible top was down, and in his impatience, he had left the door standing open on the driver's side.

Paul waved once. She waved back, waiting at the door until he had driven away.

The drawing room door was open now. Minnie had been unable to restrain her curiosity any longer once Paul was gone from the scene. Michael Forrest was looking considerably less excited, although far from calm. His head snapped around as Carol came in, but when he saw it was her again, he looked disappointed.

'Who are you?' he demanded.

'I . . . ' she began hesitantly, looking to

Wilfred for guidance.

'It's all right, my dear,' Wilfred said. 'This is Miss Andrews, a friend of ours and of Isabella's. Carol, dear, this is Mr. Forrest, Isabella's fiancé. He has come here looking for her.'

'Which brings us back to my question — where is she?' Mr. Forrest said again, ignoring Carol and the introduction. 'I demand to see her.'

'I'm afraid where she is at the moment will take some explaining,' Wilfred said. 'Carol, perhaps you had better leave this to me, if you don't mind.'

'If you like,' she said. 'If you will excuse me, please, Mr. Forrest, it was nice meeting you.'

Wilfred again closed the drawing room door after her. As she started up the stairs, she heard footsteps and looked back to see both Harley, the butler, and the chauffeur let themselves into the drawing room.

Mr. Forrest had certainly looked as if he might very well get violent. Wilfred might well want the servants on hand just in case.

It crossed her mind to wonder why Michael Forrest should be looking for his fiancée here, if she was abroad. One would think that surely he would know where she was.

She shrugged; she had been hired for a particular purpose, and in fact her job was finished now. It remained only to pack her things and return to New York. And to Paul Winters.

She began to pack her things, eager now to be done with Hale House. She hoped Mr. Forrest would not keep Wilfred and Minnie occupied for long, and thus delay their intended departure. Now that she had made the decision to go to Paul in New York, she wanted to be on her way.

She was nearly finished with her packing when she heard the sound of a car's engine, a loud, powerful roar. She went to the window and pulled aside a curtain. Mr. Forrest's red sports car was just pulling away from the house, down the long drive that twisted its way to the highway. He had taken the time to put the top up, which suggested that he must have calmed down from his earlier excited state.

So he was gone. Presumably Wilfred had in some way satisfied him. Had he told the young man the truth?

Probably she would never know. So be it. The most important thing now was that Minnie and Wilfred would soon be getting ready to leave. In an hour or so she would be on her way back to Manhattan, to Paul.

She put the last item into the suitcase and closed the lid firmly — and paused, glancing around the room. Paul had asked her about her cell phone, but now it occurred to her that she hadn't seen it since she had come in.

Maybe she had taken it downstairs and left it there. It certainly was not here.

6

The house was quiet when she came down an hour later. She was thirsty, but she did not feel inclined to ring for Mrs. Green,

As she turned in the direction of the kitchen, she had just a glimpse of Mrs. Green disappearing through a door that clicked shut after her.

At first she thought nothing of what she had seen, except perhaps a sense of relief that she would not have to encounter the unpleasant woman.

She was at the door to the kitchen when the significance of what she had just seen occurred to her. Mrs. Green had been going into the east wing of the house. She knew from the floor plans that Wilfred had sketched for her that the east wing had originally been used primarily for entertaining.

'It contains several guest suites and even a large ballroom,' he had explained.

'But that wing is never used anymore. It's kept closed off, in fact. There was a bit of water damage a few years ago and some of the flooring needs repairs, but it seemed extravagant to keep that wing open and repaired. No one goes there, and you needn't either.'

Now she wondered what errand might have called Mrs. Green into that unused part of the house. Idle curiosity led her to the same door through which Mrs. Green had passed a moment before. It was locked.

Perhaps the housekeeper was conducting a clandestine affair with one of the menservants. The idea of the dour housekeeper involved in romantic intrigue with the chauffeur made her smile.

She found the refrigerator well stocked. Considering that Wilfred had told her the family did not often use the house, she could not help thinking that the servants who stayed on here apparently lived rather well.

There was an ample supply of bottled soft drinks. She helped herself to one and was just pouring it over ice in a glass when an unexpected sound behind her made her jump. She whirled about to find the housekeeper behind her, just inside the room. She was bearing a tray on which were several dirty dishes.

'What are you doing here?' Mrs. Green demanded.

'I — I was thirsty,' Carol stammered. 'I sort of helped myself.'

'So I see.' Mrs. Green set her tray down upon the counter with a loud bang and a rattle of china. Carol moved at once toward the door. As it swung shut behind her, she was relieved to be out of the room and away from the icy stare of the housekeeper.

Wilfred was just coming down the stairs. 'Minnie is upstairs packing our bags,' he greeted her. 'We should be able to leave in a short while.'

'I'm glad, frankly,' she said. 'It will be a relief to get back to my own little apartment, and especially back to being just me. I would like to talk to you for a moment about something, if I may.'

'Of course.' He motioned toward the library. As they went in, he said, 'I hope that unfortunate incident with Mr. Forrest didn't upset you.'

'I did wonder why he was looking for Isabella here, but I truly didn't consider it any of my concern.'

Wilfred had gone to the bar and was mixing himself a martini. He spoke to her over his shoulder. 'To be perfectly honest, she led him to believe she was coming here. He's quite in love with her, poor chap, insanely, jealously so. And she is not in love with him. One of those situations, you see.'

'How unpleasant for him.' She thought of that wild-eyed young man. 'I saw him driving away.'

He looked startled. 'Did you? Mr. Forrest?'

'Well, I suppose so. The little red sports car, yes?' She shrugged. Really, she wasn't all that interested in Mr. Forrest.

Wilfred came across the room, sipping his drink tentatively, to sit near the chair she had chosen.

'Now then, what is it you wished to discuss with me?'

'I'm going to meet Paul in New York,'

she said, the words coming out in a rush. 'I thought it only right to let you know. And I intend to tell him the truth.'

'I take that to mean you have not told him yet?'

'No, certainly not. I thought it only fair to wait until I was completely finished here. But I will tell him then.'

Wilfred only regarded her in silence over the rim of his martini glass, his face impossible to read.

'Of course,' she went on, finding his silence a bit awkward, 'I'll try to persuade him to keep that knowledge to himself. I see no reason why he should feel obligated to say anything to anyone else.'

To her relief, Wilfred seemed unconcerned by her decision. 'My dear,' he said, giving her a smile that was almost paternal, 'I'm sure it could not possibly harm anything now. We have accomplished our purpose, so to speak. And I think you are wise to want to be honest with your young man. Good relationships must be built on trust.'

'I'm so glad you feel that way,' she said with relief.

He got up from his chair. 'And now, if there's nothing more, perhaps you will excuse me, I shall see McCullogh about bringing the car around to the front door. We will be leaving in just a few minutes.'

'I'll be ready.' Not until he had gone out did she remember she had meant to ask him if he had seen her missing cell phone. She walked about the room, looking at places where she might have put it down, but it was nowhere to be seen. Nor was it in the dining room or the drawing room.

Perhaps Minnie had seen it lying about and had put it somewhere out of the way. She decided she would go ask her about the phone. Anyway, Minnie was certain to be packing, and she could offer to give a hand, which would give her an excuse for a visit, and she could ask casually about her phone, without sounding as if she were accusing anyone of misplacing it.

The door to Minnie's room was closed. In her euphoric state of mind, she did not wait for an invitation to come in.

Minnie was not packing at all. She was reclining in a largish chaise lounge, her feet, in embroidered slippers, propped up comfortably. In one hand she held a cigarette and in the other a paperback book with a lurid cover that she had obviously been reading when interrupted. When Carol came in, she sat forward, an alarmed look on her face,

'What do you want?' Minnie demanded sharply.

'I came to see if I could help you with your packing.' It sounded altogether foolish because she had only to look around the room to see that Minnie was not engaged in packing. As foolish as her explanation sounded, she thought asking about her missing cell phone would be even less welcome.

Minnie put the paperback book aside and brought the cigarette to her lips. Behind its veil of smoke, Carol watched something happen to Minnie's face. It was not merely a change of expression. Rather, it was as if a mask had dropped into place. Her scowl became a smile obviously intended to be warm and friendly, and succeeding in neither.

'How sweet of you,' she said, bringing

her feet a trifle too slowly to the floor. 'You know, I've been thinking since we got here, I wish I had a daughter like you, honey. I really do.'

Carol stood in embarrassed silence, her hand still on the knob.

'Ah, here you are.' Wilfred's voice behind her gave her a bad start. She must have shown it because he said, when she whirled about, 'Did I frighten you? I am sorry.'

She gave a nervous little laugh and tried to recover her poise. At least his arrival had spared any lengthening of the scene between her and Minnie.

'I'm afraid I have some distressing news,' he said. 'It seems as if we are not going to be leaving as soon as we thought. It turns out there is some trouble with the car and McCullogh has taken it into town to have it worked on.'

'Oh,' was all Carol could say. Her sense of disappointment was as keen as if he had struck her a blow.

'Ah, that's too bad, isn't it?' Minnie said from the chaise. 'What a shame.'

But you already knew, Carol very

nearly said. *That's why you hadn't even started your packing, because you knew we wouldn't be leaving yet.*

She looked from one to the other of them. They were watching her in a seemingly sympathetic way.

Carol suddenly thought it best if she too put on a mask. 'I suppose if we must stay, we must,' she said, smiling. 'Is there any suggestion of how long it will be?'

Wilfred sighed. 'I'm afraid not. Hopefully it will be cleared up shortly, and we will get away this afternoon, but we may as well be prepared for the worst. It may be tomorrow. They may not be able to fix the difficulty, they may not have the parts . . . there's no telling.'

'I guess I may as well get comfortable then,' Carol said. 'I think I'll curl up with a book.'

'Good idea,' Minnie said. She seemed satisfied with that and picked up her novel again.

'Yes,' Wilfred said. 'The library has plenty to offer. Make yourself at home, please. Meanwhile, I'll tell Mrs. Green to plan lunch.'

Carol started from the room. 'Oh,' Wilfred said, thinking of something else. 'I believe I mentioned to you before but it bears repeating — best avoid the east wing of the house. It hasn't been kept up. There is some bad flooring, as a result of leakage, and a chandelier in one of the rooms is threatening to come down on somebody's head.'

'How odd,' Carol said before she thought. 'I saw Mrs. Green going into the east wing just a short while ago.'

'You must have been mistaken,' Wilfred said. 'She knows it is not safe there.'

'Perhaps I was,' Carol said quickly. 'All those doors, they do look alike, don't they?'

Wilfred shrugged again. 'Or perhaps she had some errand that would take her there. She may store things in that wing, for all I know. I leave the housekeeping entirely in her hands.'

Minnie sighed and settled back into the chaise again.

'Well, I'll see you at lunch, then,' Carol said. She gave them a final, parting smile, and left, making her way along the hall and down the stairs.

She suddenly felt very much concerned. Since she had come here, she had been playing a part. Now, her play-acting over, she was herself again, and she had realized that Wilfred and Minnie had been play-acting as well. They were no more real than she had been as Isabella. In some way, for some reason she could not even fathom, they were trying to deceive her.

She went back to the library and to the bookcases. She pulled out a volume of Dickens — *The Haunted Man and The Ghost's Bargain*. She settled herself into a chair, adjusting the light from a floor lamp, and began to read.

'Everybody said so. Far be it from me to assert that what everybody says must be true. Everybody is, often, as likely to be wrong as right.'

She let the pages fall closed over her fingers. How true Mr. Dickens' words were. If the people who had recently been to Hale House were questioned, each of them would say that he had seen Isabella Hale. Everybody would say so. Yet they would all of them be in error.

That was no tribute, however, to her skill as an actress. They had all seen exactly what they had expected to see when they had come here. It was they who had deceived themselves. They had seen what they believed they saw.

And she? What had she seen simply because she had expected to see it?

With a sigh, she put the book aside and gazed pensively toward the window.

Perhaps she was only being fanciful. Minnie hadn't begun her packing when she was expected to do so, and Mrs. Green had gone into the forbidden east wing and come back later with a dinner tray of dirty dishes.

Perhaps she was only seeing what she expected to see. Because she was unhappy over the delays, she had looked for more fuel for her unhappiness and had found it in what might very well be utterly innocent circumstances.

She picked up her book again and tried once more to read. She was still struggling with Dickens when Wilfred came to tell her lunch was ready.

Mrs. Green served a lunch that was more than ample — especially, Carol thought, considering the short notice that she had been given. While they ate, Wilfred informed her sadly that there was still no word regarding the car.

'It looks as if we may be stranded until tomorrow,' he said. 'Although of course I have given instructions that it must be done as quickly as possible. I hope you will be able to occupy yourself in the meanwhile.'

After lunch she abandoned her book and decided instead to go out for a stroll. She walked around the house, following the terraces of flagstone, and remembering that she and Paul had walked here only yesterday.

She wished he were with her now. The hours would not seem to drag so then. The car had seemed to be running just fine when she had arrived here in it. Surely if it had been something major . . .

She sighed. There was no use stewing about it, and nothing she could do but wait till the work was done.

She had come to the rear of the house.

This was where she had stood with Paul, looking out over the hills. Her eyes followed the winding path of the drive- way, becoming thinner and thinner as it twisted its way down through the woods, disappearing into patches of green, only to reappear a bit further on, thinner still.

A flash of red below caught her eye. It was a mere glimmer, lost in a sea of green tree tops. She tried to find it again but she had moved slightly even as she had spot- ted it, and that slight difference had lost it to her view. She took a step back and saw it again, a tiny speck of scarlet.

She watched for several minutes and the splash of red did not move at all in that time. It was like a tiny gem, gleaming through the blur of leaves.

It could be anything, she decided, losing interest. Most likely it was a bank of wildflowers of some sort.

She went restlessly indoors again, thinking that the day was proving to be a very long one indeed.

The afternoon stretched on, seeming an eternity. Minnie remained out of sight, presumably absorbed in her book. Wilfred joined Carol in the afternoon and, seeing that she looked at loose ends, suggested a game of cribbage.

The time passed.

Minnie joined them for dinner. Again, a surprisingly sumptuous repast, considering that it could not have been planned in advance. Minnie's determined good cheer only added to Carol's sense of gloom.

She was genuinely grateful when it was finally time to go to bed. In fact she went up early. Her bags were still sitting where she had left them near the door, neatly packed. She had to open one and remove her nightdress.

She remembered the missing cell phone and searched the suitcases again, with no success. She looked around the room, frowning, trying to recall when she had last seen it. In her mind's eye, she saw it lying atop the baroque dresser by the window.

There had been more help in the house then, temporary people — from the town nearby, Wilfred had told her. Perhaps one of the maids, seeing it, had stolen it.

She made a mental note to call the

phone company and cancel the service when she got back to town. She sighed as she got into bed. At least she surely had only this night to sleep through, and when she next awakened, she would be all but on her way to Paul.

She was mistaken in that assumption, however, for when she next awakened, it was still night. She was awakened by a scream, a high, keening wail of terror that brought her from her bed in one swift, frightened moment. She stared at the clock on the nightstand. Not quite three a.m.

She shivered, listening, in the cold darkness. No sound came in the wake of that single scream except for the timid rattling of a window pane in the night breeze — but the night air seemed to be filled with menace.

She jumped out of bed and stood in frightened indecision, afraid. At length she shrugged her robe about her shoulders the floor cool upon her bare feet and let herself quietly into the hall.

Nothing stirred. No sounds disturbed the quiet. The only light was the moonlight filtering through the high windows at each end of the hall. The shadows shifted as a bank of clouds moved in front of the moon.

Who had screamed? And where and why? It had been a woman, she was certain of that.

She took three faltering steps in the direction from which she thought the scream had come, and stopped.

The east wing. Yes, surely it had come from there, and that made sense, did it not? Hadn't Wilfred warned her that it was dangerous to go there? Someone, disregarding the warnings, must have gone into that part of the house, just as Mrs. Green had done earlier in the day, and had been hurt. Perhaps Mrs. Green herself had fallen victim to those rotting floorboards.

She began to run in the direction of the east wing. One of the shadows separated itself from the others, suddenly stepping into her path. It happened too quickly for her to respond. She ran into the arms of a man, who seized her firmly.

She tried to scream as that other woman had screamed, but nothing came from her taut throat.

She fought against the hands holding her, fear giving her a strength she would not ordinarily have possessed. Her flight had given her momentum, too, so that she broke from the grip that would have held her and instead fell noisily, painfully, to the floor.

She looked up and saw who was standing over her in the dim light. 'Wilfred,' she managed to croak.

'What on earth?' he exclaimed aloud, staring at her with bewildered eyes. 'Why in the name of heaven are you running about in the halls like this, in the middle of the night? You scared the dickens out of me.'

He stooped down, putting an arm about her trembling shoulders. 'Good Lord,' he said, staring into her face at closer range. 'You look like you've been scared out of your wits. Was someone in your bedroom? If there's an intruder I'll ring for Harley . . . '

'No . . . that woman . . . the scream . . . I thought . . . ' But she couldn't get her words together in the right order.

'What woman?' he asked. 'A scream, did you say? I don't know what you're talking about.'

'I heard a scream,' she said calmly, though she thought the explanation was surely superfluous, since he could hardly have helped hearing it himself. It was not the sort of sound one could just not notice.

It seemed, however, that was exactly what had happened. 'Did you?' he asked, looking at her curiously. 'When?'

'Just now. A moment ago. It came from over there.' She pointed in the general direction in which she had been running.

Wilfred gave his head a confused shake. 'I have been right here, in the hall, for five or ten minutes. And I have not heard a thing, not until you came along and scared me out of seven years of growth.'

She stared at him in disbelief. 'But you must have heard that woman's scream. It was . . . it was horrible.'

He reached out to put a gentle hand upon her arm. 'Are you quite sure you didn't just have a bad dream?'

'No,' she said quickly. But was she

sure? She had been sound asleep . . .

'We've all been keyed up all day. That's why I was out here in the hall, because I couldn't sleep and I didn't want to wake Minnie with my pacing about.'

As he spoke he coaxed her gently along the hall, in the other direction, back toward her room.

'It was so real,' she said. 'Maybe we ought to have a look, just in case.'

'That part of the house isn't safe in broad daylight. It would not be wise of us to go poking about in there at night.'

'But if there really was someone there, and she was hurt . . . '

'Look, now, you said it was a woman who screamed, did you not? Well, the only women in the house now are you and Minnie and Mrs. Green. You're here with me, so that lets you out — unless you're a ghost. You are the real Carol Andrews, aren't you?' He cocked an eyebrow but she found it impossible to be amused at that moment. 'And I know that Minnie is in bed, I left her there sleeping peacefully. And I might point out, your scream does not seem to have aroused her. That leaves only Mrs. Green. If you insist, we can go and check her room.' He glanced at his wrist. 'Good Heavens, it's nearly three in the morning. I don't imagine she will like being wakened over someone's bad dream.'

They had reached her door. Carol hesitated. It was true, she had been asleep. She could not be one hundred percent certain now that she hadn't dreamed it after all. And if Wilfred had been here, in the hall, and he hadn't heard it, then surely she *must* have dreamed it?

Still she hesitated, reluctant to give the matter up.

'All right,' he said at length. 'But I am simply not going to take you into that part of the house at night. If you broke your neck I would never forgive myself. But if it will make you feel any better, I myself will get a flashlight and go have a quick look-see. Would that do?'

'It would, yes. Thank you.'

'All right. You go on back to bed now, scoot. I will have a look, I promise. But if you hear another scream, it will be me, falling through those rotted stairs.'

She gave him a sickly smile in response to his chuckle, and slipped into her room.

'Now straight to bed,' he called through the closing door.

He waited a long moment, listening, but there was no sound from her room. Finally, with a backward glance over his shoulder, he went hurriedly but silently down the hall. He went without pausing past his own bedroom, all the way to the end of the corridor.

The east wing formed an 'L' off to the right. Tall carved doors literally shut off the entire wing, as they did on the first floor. The wing had never been used except for entertaining, and at other times it had been far more practical to be able to close it off.

The doors were unlocked. He opened them and looked in. Minnie stood just beyond, her arms folded across her immense bosom.

'It's all right,' he said in a low voice. 'She's gone back to bed.'

'We ought to have locked her in,' Minnie said petulantly. 'That's what I wanted to do, if you'll remember.'

He said nothing. When she came into the main hall with him, he locked the doors after her. She did not wait for him but went on slippered feet toward their bedroom. He followed in her wake. He looked like a man with a great deal on his mind, and none of it pleasant.

They reached their room and went in. Silence descended. The only movement was at the door to Carol's room. It had been opened a mere crack. It closed softly now, and a moment after her bed gave a faint creak of protest as she got into it again.

7

Carol woke feeling awful. At least it was morning this time, and she woke without the benefit of screams, but she had scarcely slept at all since the disturbance and her encounter with Wilfred.

She had lain for an hour or more in bed, unable to slow her whirling thoughts. It was close to dawn when she had at last drifted off into a fitful and dream-haunted sleep.

The morning sun filtered through the closed draperies. She threw back the covers and went to the window, opening the drapes wide and sending streams of dust motes dancing.

Why had Wilfred lied to her about where Minnie had been? Or, had he really lied? Perhaps he had thought she was in bed, only to discover, when he went to search the east wing — as he had promised her he would — that Minnie was there, for whatever purpose? And was it Minnie, then, who had screamed?

If that were really the case Wilfred would certainly tell her so when they next met. There would be explanations around the breakfast table and perhaps they would all three of them laugh.

She dressed quickly and hurried down for breakfast. Wilfred and Minnie were already there, seated at the table, a wordless Mrs. Green serving them. Carol sat, and began dutifully to eat the breakfast Mrs. Green quickly placed before her.

No explanations for the night's events were forthcoming. Minnie looked surly and withdrawn. Wilfred seemed to have nothing on his mind more important than the bacon and eggs he was consuming.

'I trust you slept better after our night-time rendezvous,' he said.

'To be honest, I slept better before,' she said.

'Huh?' Minnie said, rousing herself. 'What's this? You two having clandestine meetings behind my back?'

It seemed to Carol that her amusement was a bit forced. 'I thought I heard a woman screaming during the night,' she said, in a cool voice.

'Lordy,' Minnie said, her amusement morphing into an equally unconvincing show of alarm. She turned from Carol to her husband. 'Did you hear it too, Willie?'

'Not a peep,' he said.

It did not seem as if they intended to offer her any explanations.

'But you did go to investigate,' she prodded Wilfred gently.

'Yes, I did. Very briefly, I will admit, but I found nothing amiss, no one in distress, not a single dead body. What's more, I sent Mrs. Green — who, I should say, insists she heard nothing either — to take another look this morning, in case I had missed anything. She tells me she found nothing but a great deal of dust and another section of flooring that has become unsafe. I suppose we are going to have to do something about that part of the house.' He shook his head sadly at the burden of his responsibilities.

'It sounds to me,' Minnie said to Carol, 'as if Mrs. Green's fish chowder didn't sit right with you.'

Carol finished her breakfast in silence.

The house seemed more oppressive than ever this morning. She had a sense of being trapped, a prisoner in this isolated mansion. That was ridiculous, wasn't it?

The morning was clear and sunny. She went outside, walking aimlessly. At least she felt better outside, away from the shadows and gloom of the house.

She decided to walk the rest of the way around the house, to the point where you could see the driveway curving down into the valley. When she got there, she would surely see the silver Mercedes coming up the long, narrow road.

She walked slowly, her hands in the pockets of her skirt. At the terrace, she looked about idly first, before casting a casual glance down the hill.

Nothing moved. No car inched its way along the snake-like drive. She bit her lip and looked away.

Something caught her eye as she did so — a flash of red. She looked back. Yes, there it was again, just where it had been yesterday. A thought popped into her mind, an idea of what it was, but it seemed too incredible . . .

She traced the line of the road running down from the closest point she could see, running down the hill, twisting, until it passed near the patch of red, just before a large overhang of white rock.

It was no more than a mile away. Not a long walk on a pleasant day, especially when she had nothing else to do with herself.

She went around the house again, to where the drive swept up to the entry way, and began to walk along the drive. It was graveled in front of the house, the gravel neatly raked, but a little farther along the drive was only a beaten down dirt road.

It seemed to be farther than her original guess. It was nearly forty minutes later before she reached her destination.

She nearly went by it, in fact, because it was back some distance from the road, carefully hidden in a patch of thick brush, but a flash of light on a chromium surface gave her the clue. She left the road and walked in that direction. The brush by the roadside had been crushed down and then pushed back into place to conceal the trail, but only a few feet in the tire tracks were unhidden.

It was easy to follow their twisting course about a patch of shrubbery and a few trees, until she reached the place where the red sports car was parked. Michael Forrest's red sports car. Isabella's fiancé.

The car was empty. The door was unlocked. The air inside the car was hot and musty, as if it had been closed up for a while. She rummaged in the glove box and found the registration papers, which only confirmed that this was Mr. Forrest's car.

Obviously it meant that Mr. Forrest had not left. He had only tried to make it seem that he was leaving. But why go to such a pretense?

It seemed to her that there could be only one logical explanation. Young Mr. Forrest had only one conceivable reason for lingering here at Hale House — or, for that matter, for being here at all. He wanted to see Isabella Hale. And if he were still here, he must believe that

Isabella was here as well. Wilfred had simply not convinced him that Isabella was abroad.

But she was . . . wasn't she? Because that was the whole point of her being here. Or had Wildred and Minnie lied to her?

Her skin crawled. That scream in the night . . . what if it had been real, and Wilfred and Minnie had lied to her about that as well? But, then, whose voice had that been?

Could it have been Isabella's?

She got out of the car, shutting the door again firmly, and went back to the road. She stood at its edge, looking first up at Hale House, towering above, and then down the road, in the direction of the town they had passed through on the way here.

If she really believed that something was amiss at Hale House — if she thought for even a minute that Isabella Hale was there, a prisoner — she had only to walk the other way, down toward the distant town, and . . .

And what? Tell them that she thought she had heard a scream in the night, which she might actually have dreamed? That she had found a lovesick suitor's car parked nearby, concealed in the woods, a car belonging to a young man who had been nearly hysterical when she had met him, who believed, perhaps not too rationally, that Isabella Hale was in the house on the hill? That she herself, Carol Andrews, had been hired to impersonate Isabella, in order to donate a large sum of money to a children's foundation?

It was all too incredible. But now the very woods around her suddenly seemed ominous and threatening.

A sound behind her startled her. Something was moving, fast, through the bushes. She turned and caught a single, brief glimpse of a man scrambling down a small bank. He disappeared into a ravine. He was coming toward her.

Mr. Forrest, she thought. Of course. She stood her ground and waited. Irrational Mr. Forrest might be, but there were things she thought he might be able to tell her and things she might tell him, too, as a possible ally. She might well need an ally.

It was not Forrest, however, charging through the woods toward her. A moment later Harley, the butler from the house, came into view, climbing out of the ravine and walking swiftly, purposefully toward her. She felt the prickling of her skin again.

His look of surprise was so artificial that she could only wonder that he bothered to pretend at all. 'Why, hello, Miss,' he greeted her, stopping a few feet away. 'I was just out for a stroll. I never expected to see you here.'

He was breathing hard from his mad rush down the hill, shunning the road to take short cuts instead, to reach her all the sooner. He had hardly been out taking a stroll, as he put it. He had come after her, she was sure of it.

She realized she would have been visible from the house. It had never occurred to her that there was any reason to conceal herself.

Apparently she had been seen and Harley had come after her, in a big hurry. The realization made her wary. Instinctively she took a few steps away from him, into the road. She stopped herself from glancing down the road, toward town. For a fleeting few seconds she had thought of making a dash for it, but common sense told her she could hardly outrun him, and she would only be giving her hand away. Better to fight his pretense with pretense of her own.

'I was just out for a stroll myself,' she said. She let her eyes glide past him, in the direction of the parked car. Had he seen it? From here it would be difficult to spot unless you were looking for it as she had been. The butler had been in a hurry to reach her, so he might not have noticed a bit of red showing through the trees. Which meant that, if Mr. Forrest were around here somewhere, his secret might still be safe . . . and she might still have him as a possible ally.

Best to get away from this spot, before Harley made any discoveries. 'I suppose I had better start back,' she said, trying to sound casual.

'Yes,' he said, sounding relieved. Maybe he really had expected her to try to run away. He moved toward her. 'I had best walk back with you, Miss. These woods are not altogether safe to be out in.'

'No, I suppose they aren't.' She saw him glance back toward the parked car. Not a casual glance, either, but intent, seeking. So he knew it was there. He was looking to see if it could be detected from where she had been standing. Which possibly meant he didn't know that she had already discovered it. But if he knew it was there, Wilfred must know as well, mustn't he?

When he glanced back at her, however, she saw in his eyes that he knew she had discovered it already. She could almost hear the wheels turning in his mind, wondering if he should mention it, and how.

'No,' he agreed with her remark. 'There are wild animals around.'

He fell into step beside her. He was escorting her back to the house, plain and simple, and they both knew it, although neither of them wanted to acknowledge it. She wondered what he would do if she just stopped in her tracks and refused to go on? Or if she actually turned around and started toward town. She felt sure he would not let her go. If need be, he would probably throw her over his burly shoulder and carry her back to Hale House.

'What sort of animals?' she asked.

'Huh?' He looked at her, clearly surprised.

'You said there were animals in the woods. What kinds of animals? Bears?'

'Yes. Bears. I'm sure there are bears around here.'

They finished their stroll without further conversation. He was sweating profusely by the time they reached the house. He had, she guessed, run nearly all the way downhill to reach her fast, and she had deliberately come up the hill at a fast clip.

When they reached the front terrace she could not resist saying, 'You must be in remarkable condition, with all this brisk walking. Do you do this every day?'

'Not every day, Miss,' he said, opening the front door for her, breathing laboriously. That fact, at least, gave her a certain amount of pleasure.

She believed in taking the bull by the horns. She went immediately in search of Wilfred and found him in the library, poring over a set of ledgers — household accounts, she supposed.

'Yes?' Wilfred looked pleased to see her, as he always did, and not at all as if she had just interrupted him at work.

'I've been out for a walk,' she said. 'Down the hill.'

'Yes, I know.' He closed the ledger, looking down at it briefly, as if a little embarrassed. 'I saw you. From the window just there. I'm afraid you will think it a bit forward of me, but I sent Harley after you.'

His frank admission took some of the wind out of her sails. 'May I ask why?'

'You are a city girl. I was a bit concerned that the woods might not be entirely safe for you. I have said before, I do feel a responsibility for your safety while you are here. After all, you would not be here if I had not asked you.'

'Harley seemed to think I was in

danger of being set upon by bears.'

He chuckled. 'Well, I personally don't think there are any around here, but the natives tell stories; I can't say how fanciful they might be. Nevertheless, however slim the chances, I cannot just ignore them where you are concerned, can I? A young woman unfamiliar with the woods might easily stumble, hurt herself. I am sorry if you feel I have treated you like a helpless child. I assure you I had your safety at heart.'

She could hardly erupt in anger after such a humble apology.

'I should apologize for being so ungrateful,' she said, feeling a little foolish.

'Wilfred, I . . . ' Minnie came into the room behind her and, seeing her there, stopped. 'Why, hello, dear,' she said, looking quite cheerful. 'Been out for a walk, have you?'

The question jarred. Wilfred hadn't just happened to see her from the window and send Harley after her. Minnie had known too, it seemed, and had no doubt been consulted. And Minnie's casual visit just now was a 'checking up' to assure herself that everything had been handled smoothly.

'Yes, I did go for a walk.' She thought about the red car parked below. But if Harley knew it was there, Wilfred and Minnie must know as well — or would, as soon as Harley had the chance to tell them. So she had nothing to gain by remaining silent about it. On an impulse, she said, 'I did come across something rather peculiar while I was out.'

'Really?' Wilfred did not look in the least concerned.

'I found Mr. Forrest's car, hidden in the woods, back a ways from the road.'

'Mr. Forrest?'

'You remember, Willie,' Minnie supplied. 'Isabella's so-called fiancé. That crazy-acting young man. He was up here yesterday, looking for her.'

'Oh, yes, of course, that young man. But he's gone. He left right after that hysterical scene yesterday. Didn't you say you had seen him driving away?'

'I did, yes.'

'Still, you say you found his car? Where?'

She told him the general location. She had the distinct impression that this was not news to him.

'How peculiar,' he said. 'I thought he had gone. He must not have believed me when I told him Isabella wasn't here.'

'I don't like the idea of his hanging around,' Minnie said with a little shiver. 'It makes me nervous to think of him snooping around. Why, for all we know, he might even be in the house this very minute. And I don't think he looked like he was altogether right in the head.'

'Leave this to me, my dears,' Wilfred said. 'If Mr. Forrest is still hanging around for whatever reason, it shall be taken care of. First, let's look into the matter of his car.'

He touched a button on the desk. After a moment, Harley the butler appeared again.

'Miss Andrews believes she has found a strange car hidden along the road up to the house,' Wilfred told him. 'About a mile and a half down. Is that right?' He shot a glance at Carol.

'About where you found me a little

while ago,' Carol said. She watched the butler carefully. She was certain that he already knew the car was there, but if so he said nothing of it to Wilfred.

'Look into it, will you?' Wilfred went on. 'Take McCullogh with you. If this man is snooping around somewhere, I want to know about it.'

Watching Harley go, Carol had an eerie sense of unreality, as if everything that happened was only part of a play being acted on a stage.

Wilfred saw her frown and misread it. 'Now, don't either of you ladies worry yourselves over this. It shall all be taken care of, I promise you.'

There seemed to be no alternative but to smile and thank him for being the strong, protective male — since that was the role he was playing in this staged drama.

She was not really surprised by what happened at lunch. Once again Mrs. Green had provided very well, considering that she had known they would be staying on this long. And considering, too, that with no car available, she had no access to a market. The fresh greens in the salad, Carol thought, might have been purchased this very morning.

It was Minnie who brought up the subject of Mr. Forrest.

'Did Harley and McCullogh find that car?' she asked, chewing on a bit of lettuce. 'The one that Carol here thought she saw.'

Wilfred put his fork aside, 'As a matter of fact, no, they did not,' he said.

'But it was there,' Carol insisted. 'I didn't just imagine it.'

'Oh, yes, they confirmed some car had been there, but had left recently. It looks as if Mr. Forrest must have satisfied himself after all that Isabella was not here, and simply went away. I doubt he will be troubling us again.'

'I still don't like the idea of his prowling around here without our knowing it.' Minnie gave a little shudder.

Carol said nothing.

'Doesn't the whole business give you the willies, dear?' Minnie asked her.

'Yes, it does,' Carol said, and stabbed a bit of very fresh tomato with her fork.

Since no one had brought up the subject of car repairs, she asked, when lunch was nearly finished, 'And the car? Is it working again?'

'I'm afraid,' Wilfred said, looking genuinely sorry, 'that we are still very much marooned. It seems the mechanic had to send away for a part. They are expecting it any moment, McCullough tells me.'

'What was the part?' Carol asked.

The question, so completely unexpected, caught Wilfred at a rare loss. After a long and awkward silence he said, 'I have no idea, actually, although I'm sure they did tell me. I'm afraid I have no aptitude for things mechanical.'

'Lordie, neither have I,' Minnie agreed quickly. 'I can't tell the front end of a car from the back unless I'm sitting in it. Can you?' She fixed sharp eyes on Carol.

She had only asked her question about the part to see the reaction it produced. And it had produced exactly the reaction she had expected.

'I'm afraid not,' she answered Minnie's question. The sharp eyes watching her grew a bit less concerned.

When she went out into the hall, Carol had a glimpse of Mrs. Green. The housekeeper was just disappearing into the east wing. Although her back was to Carol, she walked as if she were carrying something.

A tray, Carol wondered? For whom? Was there someone else in the house who was a prisoner?

As, apparently, was she.

8

She had already decided what she was going to do, and was only waiting for the right opportunity. She had it now, with Wilfred and Minnie lingering over their coffee and Mrs. Green on her mysterious errand to the east wing.

She no longer wondered what had happened to her cell phone. By now, she was convinced that Wilfred or Minnie, or even Mrs. Green, had taken it to prevent her calling anyone. It was not as if she were completely cut off from the outside world, however, the house did have phone service.

Granted, she could hardly call the local police with a lot of vague fears and suppositions. There was someone she could call, though, someone she was sure would come to her rescue. And with Paul Winters here, she felt confident that she could leave Hale House at will.

Her bedroom had no phone, although

she had found a phone jack near the nightstand. She knew of only two instruments in the house, although there might be others elsewhere. One of the phones was in Wilfred and Minnie's bedroom, she had seen it there when she went to ask Minnie about her packing.

The other phone was in the library. Wilfred apparently used that room as an office when he was here, and she had seen the phone on his desk when she had confronted him after her encounter with Harley.

She went quickly to the library. She would have liked to lock that door behind her, but she did not want to rouse any suspicions. No matter how eager he might be to see her, Paul could not reach Hale House in less than four or five hours. She did not wish to sound any alarms here in the house before then.

If he arrived unexpectedly for her, there was nothing anyone could do to prevent her from leaving with him, but if they had advance notice that she was frightened, that he was coming to get her, they would have plenty of time to do . . . whatever they might decide to do. She did not want to pursue that thought further.

In the library, she went without hesitation to the phone, lifting the receiver from its cradle. She had committed Paul's number to memory and her finger began to dial the digits without pause.

She had dialed the area code and the first three numbers before she realized that nothing was happening in response. None of the usual sounds of phone connections being made.

She clicked the button in the cradle impatiently and began to dial again. When nothing happened the second time, she realized the truth: the phone was dead.

She replaced the receiver. Of course, she should have expected this. The phone had not rung the whole time she had been here. Wilfred and Minnie almost certainly had cell phones — if not their own, then hers. They would not have left the house phone on, knowing how easy it would be for her to use it.

Fear settled about her shoulders like a mantle placed by some unseen presence.

She went quickly to the French doors and stepped out onto the terrace, gulping the air greedily, as if she had been shut up in some dark tomb and had just been set free.

Only, she wasn't free.

But why? What conceivable reason could they have for wanting to keep her here, at Hale House? She could be of no value to them. Certainly she was not being held for ransom. They knew enough about her to know that there was no one who was likely or even able to pay any ransom to set her free.

She had already performed her impersonation of Isabella. They could hardly expect to force her to perform again. And why force her anyway? If for some reason they needed a repeat performance, why not simply ask her?

Unless they meant for her to do something they knew she would object to doing, something less innocent than what she had done previously. Perhaps that had only been to set the stage for what they really wanted.

A possibility, but it still left unanswered

questions. How could they force her to perform in front of others, and prevent her from telling the truth?

She shook her head, putting a hand to one temple, and walked to the edge of the terrace, looking down. Here, earlier, she had glimpsed a flash of red that had turned out to be Michael Forrest's car.

She looked long and hard, but it was gone now, if she needed to confirm what Wilfred had said. She was sorry it was gone. However hysterical Mr. Forrest had been, he might at least have been someone for her to turn to. He certainly was not involved in any scheme with Wilfred and Minnie.

In what way would she be valuable to them, valuable enough that they would exercise deception to keep her here, a prisoner and — at least so they thought — unaware of her cage?

Or, try it on from another angle: in what way was she a threat to them?

She had impersonated Isabella Hale. That impersonation had been harmless, even worthwhile. That much was real.

Or was it? The people who had come to

dinner that evening thought they had seen Isabella Hale, making a large and worthwhile charitable donation. She, knowing of the deception, being a part of it, had thought she was helping an innocent and well-meaning couple to do a good deed. Had that too been only an illusion? She could make no sense of it.

All right, she told herself, feeling as if her head were spinning, leave it. Never mind why. The question now was what to do about it.

She came immediately to another blank wall. She could not phone. This house was isolated. She had no idea where the next nearest house was, but she could not see it from here, wherever it was. Town was several miles away. No one was going to hear her if she started screaming.

'There you are,' Minnie said, coming through the French doors from the library. 'Out getting ourselves another breath of fresh air, are we?'

She nearly confronted Minnie then and there with all of her fears, bringing everything into the open — but she checked herself. So long as they thought she was ignorant of their machinations, she might yet find a way to get free.

'It's so lovely here,' she said, the words nearly sticking in her throat.

Minnie cast an unenthusiastic glance over the view. 'I prefer the city myself. All this quiet gets on my nerves. Well, so much the better for you, though, if you like it, since it looks like we're stuck here, for a while.'

'Do you have any idea for how long?'

'You heard Wilfred. And you know what these mechanics are like, they try to make everything as complicated as possible, to justify the high prices they mean to charge.' Her eyes narrowed. 'Why? Is someone expecting you, or anything like that?'

'Not exactly. Only, well, I am a working girl. I have other assignments coming up. If I don't show up for them, people are bound to wonder.'

'When we talked to your agent, he said you were free for . . . ' Minnie caught herself and changed courses. 'When we first planned this, we didn't know how long we might need you. Your agent said you'd be free for all this week at least.'

Carol had no assignments scheduled. No one would be concerned for a few days. Paul might be, or he might think only that she had changed her mind again and wasn't coming to him after all.

'You must have talked to him a few days before we left,' she said aloud. Minnie nodded, looking increasingly unhappy with this conversation. 'He called me the day before we came up. That is, before I came up. He had a job for me. I thought I would be back by now. I have an appointment for — let me think — is it tomorrow? I'm not sure. I suppose I should go in and call . . . '

'The phone is out of order,' Minnie said quickly.

'Really? In this lovely weather?'

'Oh, I don't actually mean out of order, not like there's a line down or something. What I meant was, we had the service shut off. We were expecting to leave before this, and we don't keep it on here when we aren't in residence. An unnecessary expense, don't you see?'

'Don't you have a cell phone with you?'

Minnie's eyes narrowed again. 'No. We neither of us carry them. I guess we're just too old-fashioned.'

And how, Carol wondered, were they staying in touch with that mechanic in town?

'Look,' Minnie said after a minute, 'the real reason I came out here was to find you and ask you if you could do a big favor for me. Do you have a minute to come upstairs?'

'Of course, I'd be glad to. I've been a little at loose ends anyway.'

Wilfred was in the library. He appeared to have been looking at the accounts again — the conscientious manager.

'Us girls,' Minnie paused in the doorway to tell him, 'are going upstairs and attend to some girl business. And you aren't invited.'

'A fine thing,' Wilfred said, 'when a man is not welcome in his own bedroom.'

Minnie smiled at his pretended indignation and nudged Carol in the ribs. Carol forced a smile.

Upstairs, in her bedroom, Minnie turned on the radio first thing, finding some rock music. She turned the volume up high.

'What I wanted to talk to you about,' Minnie said, going to the closet, 'was, when we get back to the city — which we all hope will be soon — I have got this cocktail party to go to, a real high-class affair, too, and I wanted to get your advice on what to wear. You having such good taste in clothes, I mean, and being a model, and all. You don't mind helping me, do you?'

'I don't mind at all.'

Minnie rummaged through the dresses in the closet, murmuring, 'Let me see here,' and pulled out two on hangers. One was red, a blatant red silk with a straight skirt that looked too slim for Minnie's ample hips. The other was a full-skirted print, of the sort usually described as 'tropical',' and containing, it appeared at first glance, every color of the rainbow.

'What do you think?' Minnie asked. 'I sort of lean toward the print. I think it's a little younger, don't you? And the red makes me look hard.'

Carol gave them both a long, careful

look. 'I don't know. Didn't you wear some jet black earrings the first day I saw you? Think of what that red would look like with all black accessories — gloves, belt, purse . . . '

Something had changed in the last moment or so. Minnie wasn't paying attention, not to her. Her eyes were on Carol, she was smiling politely — but in actuality she was listening to something else, straining to hear . . . what?

Carol listened too, talking fast and in a lower voice that would necessitate an effort on Minnie's part to hear her

'What was that, dear?' Minnie asked. Carol was almost mumbling by now.

She heard it then, a car roaring up the hill, changing gears at the last, sharp, steep turn. Coming fast, at this precise moment perhaps because the driver had been somehow signaled (by cell phone?) that she was out of the way, where she would not see, with a radio blaring loudly to mask any sound, and 'girl talk' to distract her.

'I said, I think it sets off your hair,' Carol said aloud.

'Really? Do you think so?' Minnie looked at each of the dresses in some confusion. Clearly she hadn't any idea which one Carol had been referring to.

'It's so perfect for you. Excuse, do you mind?' Carol went to the radio and without waiting for a reply, turned the volume down low.

Carol could hear nothing from outside now. If she could just have a look-see, fast . . . she moved toward the door.

'Wait,' Minnie said, diving back into the closet again. 'There's another one here, you may as well have a look at it too. I think Wilfred favors it . . . where is it, now?' Carol had to wait until Minnie emerged from the closet, holding a dress in a ghastly shade of purple.

'I still like the other one best,' Carol said. 'You will look lovely in it.' She was out of the room before Minnie could say anything more.

She ran lightly down the stairs and out the front door before Wilfred had time to see her and try to delay her.

The drive curved around the house on the opposite side from the terraces, leading back to the garages at the rear. The door of the end stall in the garage was closed. Hadn't it been open before, like all the others? She all but ran toward the closed door.

She did not reach it though, because the driver, McCullogh, suddenly appeared, stepping into her path so that she nearly ran right into him. She stopped dead in her tracks. He was a big, powerful looking man. His small dark eyes, not entirely unfriendly, swept her up and down.

'Looking for something?'

'No, nothing in particular,' she said quickly. 'I thought I'd just look at the garage.'

'The car's not there,' he said quickly. 'It's still in town.'

'Yes, so I heard. I just thought . . . ' She stepped to the side as if to go around him.

He sidestepped also. 'You shouldn't go in there,' he said. He paused, then: 'It's dirty. It's no place for a young lady.'

She did not believe him, but she did not feel brave enough to demand that he let her pass. She felt certain that he would not let her go into the garage, even if he had to restrain her bodily. She did not want find herself in his arms, vulnerable to whatever ideas might cross his mind.

She looked past him. 'Do you live there? In the garage?'

'In the apartment above.' He grinned then, showing a broken tooth. 'Now, if you wanted to see my apartment . . . ?' He moved a step toward her. 'There's outside stairs up to it, we could . . . '

'No.' She took a step backward and managed a tremulous smile. 'Thank you. Perhaps some other time.'

It took an effort of will to turn her back on him and walk away. At the corner of the house, she glanced over her shoulder. He was still watching her.

★   ★   ★

She pleaded a headache and spent the rest of the morning in her room. She was not able to look at Wilfred or Minnie without an eerie sense of apprehension.

If the car could not be repaired promptly, why had Wilfred simply not arranged for another car? For that matter, surely the family had more than one car.

And what of her impression that a car had come up the hill to the house just a short while before, at the same time that Minnie had coincidentally invited her up to her room to consider some silly question of dresses for a future party? What of the fact that one of the garage stalls was now closed, as if concealing a car inside, and apparently was guarded by the chauffeur.

Perhaps most significant of all was her impression that she was being watched. Wilfred had explained why Harley had been sent after her when he had seen her walking down the road, but was that explanation the true one? Looking back, it seemed to her that rarely if ever had she been out of their sight.

She stood at the window in her room, turned these thoughts over and over in her mind. Beneath her the driveway was like a forbidden sweet. It was a road that led away from here, to freedom, to Paul.

Minnie came by at lunchtime to see how she was feeling. 'You haven't still got that headache, have you?'

Carol put a hand on her forehead. 'Yes, I do,' she said. Carol had a flash of inspiration. 'I feel just awful, really. Do you suppose there's any way of getting into town to see a doctor?'

Minnie looked doubtful. 'I couldn't say, off hand. Without a car, I don't know how.'

'There must be a cab company.'

'I'll talk to Wilfred.' Minnie paused on her way out of the room. 'I don't suppose if you just got up and moved around a bit . . . ?'

Carol put a hand on her abdomen and groaned softly. 'I've tried, but it's sheer torture. I'm afraid there is something really wrong.'

'I'll let Wilfred know.'

Wilfred brought a tray up shortly, with some soup and a cup of tea. 'Minnie says you're feeling poorly,' he said.

Carol had taken advantage of the interim to concoct an interesting variety of symptoms, which she recited to him.

He went away looking concerned.

Minnie was waiting downstairs for him.

'Well?' she greeted him.

'She might be faking, or she might be genuinely sick.'

'I'm not going to play housemaid to her,' Minnie said quickly and firmly. 'You know what I think ought to be done.'

'Yes, you've certainly told me often enough.' He gave a heavy sigh.

'Well, if you had any sense at all you'd go ahead and do it. You got her to think about, too.' She nodded in the direction of the east wing. 'We can't fool around with them forever.'

'Yes, yes, I know. I don't care for this any more than you do.'

'Then let's get it over with. Tonight, before something goes wrong. If one of them was to get out . . . '

'They won't,' he said sharply. He simply had not thought this far ahead when it had first begun, when he was acting upon an angry impulse, had not foreseen the course to which he was committing himself. He looked at his wife guardedly. Had she? She had fewer qualms about it all, he was well aware of that.

Perhaps she was right, he thought wearily. There was simply no alternative to what they must do.

'It has to be an accident,' he said.

'So, make it an accident. Tonight, then?'

'I'll see.' He went past her. He heard her give a little snort of disgust but he did not look back.

9

Had she been able to sustain her pretense of illness, Carol might eventually have succeeded in convincing them of its seriousness. Something came up, though, so unexpected and so hope inspiring that she immediately forgot all about her pretended malady.

She heard a car approaching the house. It was definitely the sound of an engine coming up the hill, not the powerful engine of the Mercedes but something more ordinary, laboring a bit on the grade. She forgot her pretended sickness and ran to the window.

A panel truck made the turn onto the gravel in front of the house. A delivery-man got out and, opening the rear of the truck, began to set cardboard boxes out, stacking them on a dolly.

Carol ran out of her room and down the stairs. No one was in the front hall to stop her and before anyone appeared, she was out the big front door and down the steps.

The deliveryman had gone around to the back of the house with a load of boxes, but as she came down the front steps she heard his footsteps and the squeak of wheels on the gravel as he came back to the truck.

'Hello,' she greeted him with a bright smile. 'I wonder if I could trouble you to give me a lift. Our car isn't running and I need to get into town.'

'We're not supposed to carry passengers,' he said a bit reluctantly. He looked her up and down in a man-woman way. She smiled more broadly to encourage him.

'I understand, but, really, it's rather urgent. And no one need ever know. If you like, I'll get out as soon as we reach the edge of town. I can walk the rest of the way.'

He gave her rather a dubious look, but he nodded his head. 'I guess so, lady. But I ain't got any time to wait.'

'I won't be a minute, I promise,' she said excitedly. 'I just have to grab my purse and I'll be right back. I'll be ready to go by the time you get those delivered.'

He had stacked the remaining boxes on his dolly and was starting about the house with them. 'Just make it fast, okay?' he replied without looking back.

She did indeed make it fast. She took the stairs two at a time. In her room, she did nothing but grab her purse. Her bags were half unpacked and there wasn't time to repack them. Anyway, most of the things in them were Isabella's. The few things that were hers weren't that important. At the moment, nothing seemed more important than getting away from here.

As she dashed down the stairs, she heard Minnie say, her voice booming, 'Land's sake, look at you, seems like you have right recovered.'

'I'm going,' Carol said without slowing her steps. She was closer to the front door than Minnie was and although Minnie was walking fast, Carol knew the older woman would never reach her in time to stop her. She heard the door of the van slam shut as she ran for the front door.

At the top of the steps, she paused for an instant. The truck's engine had roared to life again and the truck began to move.

'Hey,' she yelled. She took the steps in two long jumps, almost toppling over in the gravel, and ran as hard as she could after the truck.

The driver had heard her. He stopped and turned a surly look in her direction as she ran panting up to the door on the passenger's side.

She grabbed for the door handle — and found it locked.

'It's locked,' she gasped, looking up into the truck at the driver.

'Sorry, lady,' he said through the half-open window. 'I thought better of it. It's against the company rules.'

'But I have to get to town.' She rattled the handle. 'Please, I'll pay you. Anything you want.'

'Sorry,' he said, shaking his head again. 'Anyway, after what they told me about you in the kitchen . . . well, I can't take that kind of chances.'

The truck began to move again, slowly at first and then gaining speed. Then it was gone, in a shower of gravel and out of sight around the big, sweeping curve, and she remained behind, standing foolishly in the middle of the drive.

She turned dispiritedly back to the house. Minnie stood at the top of the steps, her arms folded across her bosom. She hadn't hurried down the steps after her or tried to stop her, and Carol now knew why. Minnie had known the driver wouldn't take her with him when he left. That last remark of his . . .

Of course, that was clear enough. He must have said something about her while he was in the kitchen, to Mrs. Green. Or maybe Minnie herself had been in the kitchen when he came in and mentioned the blonde woman who wanted him to drive her into town. She could not begin to imagine what they must have told him to make him change his mind so suddenly and so firmly. That she was crazy? That she was a criminal of some sort. Whatever it had been, it had certainly been enough to cause him to leave without her.

Minnie smiled down at her and there was no mistaking the look of triumph on her face, but there was something else as well, a vicious sort of pleasure that fed upon seeing another disappointed. She had never before realized what a truly nasty person Minnie was.

'Looks like you're feeling a whole lot better this afternoon,' Minnie said.

'Yes.' It was too late now to fall back upon her pretended 'illness'. 'I was going to ride into town with him.'

'So I heard. I guess he changed his mind, huh?'

Carol came up the steps, trying not to look defeated.

'Don't worry,' Minnie said, putting a heavy hand on her shoulder. 'Wilfred will take care of everything.'

Back upstairs, in her room, Carol stood at the window where she had stood only minutes before, seeing the truck pull up in front of the house.

Why were they keeping her here? What did they mean to do with her? Because it was no longer possible for her to pretend that it was in any way innocent.

★ ★ ★

She was at her window again, and night had fallen, when she saw the man.

This was after dinner. Conversation had been sparse at the evening meal with Wilfred and Minnie. Nothing was said about her attempt to leave. The incident might never have happened. Wilfred made an effort to chat, but Minnie answered him in the briefest of terms, leaving it up to Carol to respond to his efforts in a lackluster way.

When she came upstairs to her room again, Carol left her lights off and went to the window again, looking out at the night and wondering what on earth she could do about her predicament. It was then that she saw him.

What she saw at first was the glow of his cigarette when he lifted it up to his mouth as he puffed at it. Then with a sudden gesture, he threw it away. It made a graceful arc through the air before it fell to the ground where it continued to glow for a few seconds.

She saw a flash of movement where the man had been standing, partly in the shadows of the trees, but in enough of the moon's pale light to tell her that it was someone in trousers, and then he was gone.

For a moment she thought it was Wilfred, perhaps watching her window, but suddenly it came to her that she had never seen Wilfred with a cigarette.

Minnie smoked, but she had never seen Minnie in trousers. The answer came to her in a flash: Might it not be young Michael Forrest, Isabella's fiancé? Perhaps he had not gone away after all, but had only tricked Wilfred into thinking that he had by moving his car a second time. Perhaps he was still here, watching for some glimpse of Isabella.

She got a jacket to put around her shoulders and let herself out of her room. The house was quiet. If only she could make it outside without seeing the others.

That was not to be. She was halfway down the stairs when Wilfred appeared at the bottom. He looked up at her.

'Were you going out?' he asked.

'Just to the terrace. I felt restless. I thought a breath of air might do me good.'

He hesitated ever so briefly. 'Perhaps I ought to come with you. You never know what might be out there in the dark.'

'I'm sure there's no danger,' she said guardedly. 'I hadn't intended to go beyond the terrace. But thank you for offering just the same.'

'Oh, it's no trouble. I could use some air myself. I've been wrestling with the books too long.'

She resumed her descent of the stairs. 'Well, if you aren't just being kind,' she said. 'Why don't you get yourself a jacket, then, and join me?'

He took her arm in a protective fashion. 'I don't think I'll need a jacket.'

They went outside together. She was painfully aware of Michael Forrest's presence somewhere close at hand. Perhaps he was close enough that he would hear her if she cried out, and she nearly did so.

Some instinct of self-preservation, however, warned her to remain silent. If Forrest had gone away for the night and did not hear her, she would have placed herself in a dangerous position with Wilfred.

On the other hand, there was danger, too, in the possibility that Forrest, not realizing they were outside, might reveal himself at an inopportune moment.

'I think after all that it's a little cool out for comfort,' she said, talking a bit loudly and drawing the jacket close about her shoulders. She did not have to act, either. She felt genuinely chilled, although the weather was only partly responsible. 'Let's go in.'

'As you wish.' He seemed a little surprised at her abrupt change of heart, but he offered no objection to escorting her back inside the house.

'Would you like me to send Minnie up to keep you company,' he asked as she started up the stairs. 'You said that you were feeling a bit restless. Sometimes it helps to have company.'

'Oh. Thank you for the offer, but that won't be necessary. I think I'll just go to bed early.'

'Good idea,' he said, and because that sounded a bit too blunt, he added, 'I want to see you feeling your best tomorrow.'

She wondered why. It was surely not because they would be driving into New York City.

In her room, her lights still out, she went at once to her window, but there was no sign of life on the terrace, no glow of a burning cigarette. Maybe Mr. Forrest had given up finally and gone away, this time for good.

She turned from the window, surrendering to the wave of despair that broke over her. What could she do? How could she get away?

How much longer did they mean to keep her a prisoner? Did they mean to let her go at all, ever?

* * *

She was awakened again by a scream. It was briefer this time, as if cut off abruptly, but it lasted long enough that she was certain she had not dreamed it.

She did not rush out into the hall this time, sure that Wilfred or Minnie, one of the other, would be out there.

She left her lights out and got quietly out of bed, dressing in the moonlight from the window. Before she had gone to bed, she had put out a comfortable denim skirt, a plain pullover sweater, dark gray, and comfortable walking shoes. Everything essential from her purse she had shifted to the deep pocket of her skirt. At least she had learned a valuable lesson from her experience with the deliveryman. Coming back to her room for her purse had ruined her chances. If an opportunity again presented itself for her to get away, she was ready to go on the instant.

She opened her door a mere crack, listening carefully and waiting. For a while she heard nothing. She was about to step out into the hall when a door opened down the hall and she heard cautious footsteps. They were almost to her door before she realized they were coming her way; she pushed the door shut, holding the knob so there would be no telltale click.

The footsteps paused outside. She held her breath, hoping that whoever waited on the opposite side of the door would not come into her room and discover that she was not in her bed. She wished now that she had thought to bunch up the pillows to make it look as if she were still there, but she dared not now let go of the doorknob. If she did so, the latch would click into place.

After what seemed an eternity, the footsteps went away again. She cracked the door and listened. Down the hall, another door opened and closed and there was silence once more.

She made herself wait, despite her mounting excitement. As she waited, she tried to think ahead. She had awakened from sleep with two thoughts perfectly clear in her mind. First, she had to escape from Hale House — now, tonight. Some instinct told her that tomorrow would be too late. Second, before she went, she had to see into the forbidden east wing of the house. She had to know who it was that screamed in the night, and why. Someone was in terror, and she could not simply abandon whoever it was to the machinations of her jailers.

She was not yet clear just how she was going to accomplish either of those goals, only that they must be accomplished. Now, with the hall empty, the coast was clear, at least for the moment.

She opened her door and slipped out into the hall. It was dark except for the pale light filtering through the windows. Dressed as she was, in grayish clothes, she would blend easily with the shadows.

She paused thoughtfully outside her room. On an impulse, she went back to her bed and plumped up the pillows in a row down the bed. When she pulled the bedcovers up over them it looked, if someone did not examine too closely, as if she were still in bed asleep.

The hall was still empty. She could steal down the stairs and out of the house. It might be morning before they discovered she was gone, and by that time, she might have been able to reach town, or perhaps a nearby property.

For all she knew, there might be nothing at all in that other wing of the house. Even if there were, was it her responsibility? If she went now, she could probably save her own skin. If she took the time to go exploring, she might never again have an opportunity to leave. In the end, however, she had to know.

A thin border of light shone beneath

the door to Wilfred and Minnie's room and she could hear the low murmur of voices from within. She hesitated. It meant screwing up her courage to go past that door, knowing that they were awake on the other side, perhaps listening.

Her heart stopped. A board creaked under her feet, sounding like a cannon shot in the stillness of the hall. She heard someone move beyond the lighted door.

She barely had time to reach the next doorway, cringing into its shallow recess, before Wilfred's door opened. Light splashed out into the hallway. Wilfred himself stepped out, wearing an elegant robe over his pajamas.

She dared not breathe. If he looked in her direction he could scarcely fail to see her. She dared not open the door against which she was pressed, for fear of making a sound that would attract his attention.

He looked in the opposite direction, however, toward her door. He seemed undecided for a moment. Then, moving lightly and silently, he went down the hall toward her room. She heard him open her door stealthily.

At the same moment, she felt for the knob behind her, praying this door was not locked. The knob turned. She opened the door and stepped into the sheltering darkness of an unused bedroom.

Wilfred did no more than merely glance into her darkened bedroom. She heard his soft footsteps coming down the hall again and after a moment the light in the hall faded as his door was once again closed. She heard him say, as the door swung closed, 'Just a false alarm. She's safe in her bed asleep.'

She nearly cried with relief. When she had managed to get her trembling under control, she carefully opened the door and stepped once more into the hall. She moved quickly now, as if some instinct told her time was running out.

The door to the east wing of the house stood closed. If it were locked, she would have to think of some other way of gaining access to those mysterious rooms.

The knob moved when she turned it and the door came open. She tried not to think of what might be waiting in the darkness beyond. Wilfred might have been telling the truth when he told her that this part of the house was in a dangerous state of disrepair. It would be grimly ironic if she evaded Wilfred and Minnie, only to have a chandelier fall on her head.

What if someone were waiting just inside the door, watching to see who was coming in? Wilfred was accounted for, at least momentarily, and there had been someone else in his room, but she could not say with certainty that it had been Minnie. And where were Mrs. Green, and Harley, and the chauffeur?

It took an effort of will to step through the doorway into the hall beyond.

It was empty. She stood for a moment, trying to remember the floor plans she had studied earlier. She hadn't really paid much attention to this part of the house once Wilfred had told her it was not in use. But nothing Wilfred had told her seemed to have been the truth.

The hall she was in was short. It ended at the ballroom that occupied most of this wing. There were also stairs there that went down to the first floor. Along the right side of this hall were windows that, when she glanced out of them, looked down upon the front steps and the gravel parking surface. Along the left were doors, all of them closed. Guest bedrooms, she thought she recalled.

'We won't be able to use them for the guests,' Wilfred had told her, referring to the people coming to the presentation dinner, 'because that part of the house is in bad shape.'

Where, she wondered, was the evidence of the disrepair he had mentioned? Except for some dust, disturbed by footprints on the floor, it looked perfectly fine.

She went to the first of the closed bedroom doors.

It was locked. She gently rattled the knob, to no avail.

The second door was not locked. The knob turned easily in her hand and the door glided open. Beyond was quiet, and deeper shadows.

She nearly tripped over something just inside the room. She moved aside so the moonlight could fall upon whatever it was.

She saw a suitcase, a large one that looked purplish in the moonlight but was probably a deep red. By it was another, smaller one that matched, and nearby a woman's makeup case.

She really did not have to kneel and look more closely to know that the gold initials on the pieces were I.H. She traced their outlines with her fingers. It was expensive luggage, exactly what one would expect a woman of Isabella's wealth to carry, but it had a well-used look that told of a great deal of travel, and not all of it to the best places.

She tried each of the cases but they were locked. Kneeling among them, she saw what she had not seen when standing — a woman's purse.

The sight of the purse gave her a chill. Of course, it could be an old handbag. Isabella Hale must have literally dozens of purses and no doubt more than one set of luggage. Yet she found her hand was trembling when she reached for the purse.

She opened it and turned so that she could spill its contents into the pool of moonlight that fell through the open door. Lipstick in a gold and jeweled case; compact; daintily embroidered handkerchief; comb; breath freshener in a tiny atomizer; a diminutive address book in a gold-tooled case, with its own tiny pencil; a leather billfold; a credit card case . . .

She picked up the last two items, examining the billfold first.

It was quite likely that Isabella had duplicate purses, but would she have a duplicate driver's license? And would she just toss aside a purse in which the billfold contained a sheaf of paper money?

She took the bills out of their pocket and spread them in her hands. At a glance, several hundred dollars, maybe a thousand. Not very much to Isabella Hale, but surely not even the very wealthy left that much lying about in an unused bedroom as if it were small change.

The credit card case contained cards of every sort — American Express, Platinum, Visa, Master Card, Saks, Bloomingdale's.

She looked again at the contents of the purse, spilled across the floor, and spied a familiar looking folder. She picked it up with trembling hands, already sure of what she would see.

Not even the very wealthy kept duplicate passports. Inside, a familiar face looked back at her. She recognized Isabella, although the other photograph she had seen had been of a much younger woman.

Staring briefly at the photograph, she realized they were not so much different in appearance as she had once thought. Standing side by side, a person would hardly confuse one with the other, but the general resemblance was there. She could understand how Paul, having only a distant glimpse of Isabella years earlier, would not have recognized her as an imposter.

The room was too dark for her to read the passport. She went back into the hall, to the window.

Isabella had come back to the States from Kenya in mid-August. There was nothing stamped in the passport to indicate that she had left the States after that. On a forlorn impulse, she checked the year as well as the month, but no, it was this year, this August.

She closed the passport and bit hard into her lip. She had first met with Wilfred and Minnie at the end of August. She counted the days. That had been almost two weeks after Isabella had returned to the States. Isabella had been here all the time, at least somewhere in the country, when they were explaining to her in the tower suite at the hotel why they needed someone to impersonate her. Whatever their reason for wanting someone, it had not been what they told her, that Isabella was abroad.

But if Isabella were here, why would they need to hire someone to impersonate her. Unless . . .

A tremor went up and down her spine. She did not even want to finish that thought. She wanted suddenly to be out of this house, away from the couple who had brought her here. She would rather have the woods at night, with whatever dangers they held, than Hale House, with its evil schemers and its screams in the night and . . .

She could not just bolt, of course,

because there were those screams in the night, and they were still unexplained. Her initial thought when she had calculated the dates was that Isabella must have been dead, but dead women did not scream, and someone had certainly screamed, on two different occasions. Who else could it have been but Isabella?

Luckily, she went back to the bedroom that held the luggage. She had scarcely reached the safety of that room when she heard footsteps.

She pushed the door nearly closed, flattening herself against the wall so that she could see into the corridor. The beam of a flashlight played along the floor. In a moment Minnie went by, wearing a robe and slippers and her hair in curlers. She looked angry and determined about something.

She did not glance in the direction of the nearly closed door where Carol stood trembling, but went by without a pause and a moment later the door to the central hall opened and closed. A key turned in the lock with a loud, grating sound; silence returned.

Carol let out the breath she had been holding. Now, at least, she knew she was alone in this wing and did not have to be quite so cautious. She went back out into the hall.

Minnie had come from the opposite end, from the stairs there. What Carol was searching for then must be downstairs, or in the ballroom, and she need not trouble herself over the two unexplored rooms here.

At the end of the hall, she paused. To her left were the stairs going down. The curtained arches in front of her led to the galleries that overlooked the ballroom. She went through the curtains at one of the arches. Three wide steps led down. The gallery was like a miniature balcony with a railing, projecting out over the ballroom below. Although this little niche was in darkness, the ballroom itself was dimly lit.

From the railing she could see the source of the light, a single lamp burning below. It cast a pool of light on the patterned marble floor that waltzing feet had once glided across. Beyond the circle of light, the shadows hovered, inching out from the far corners that were their apparent kingdom.

She stood for a long moment at the railing, scarcely breathing, staring into the room below. She put out her hand to support herself and the wood beneath her fingers was cold and rough. The gallery had a musty, unused smell.

The lamp she had seen stood upon a table and near the table was a small bed, placed with no thought for proper appearance, since obviously only a few were intended to see it.

Upon the bed, bound hand and foot, lay a woman. From here, Carol could not tell if she were alive or dead, but even without seeing the face that was turned away from her, she felt certain the woman was Isabella Hale.

Carol turned and darted up the steps from the gallery to the hall, and down the steps that led to the floor below.

The wide double doors that went from the downstairs hall into the ballroom were closed but not locked. Clearly they had thought there was no need to lock them to hold in the bound woman on the bed.

Isabella moved as Carol burst into the room, and Carol's heart leapt up. At least she was still alive, then. The blonde head turned in her direction and Carol saw that a cloth had been tied over her mouth as well — to prevent further screams. Isabella's eyes widened in surprise.

Carol knelt down to remove the gag first. As it came away, Isabella gasped hungrily for breath. She looked pale and drawn and her eyes, that should have been bright and sparkling, were dull with fatigue.

'You're Isabella Hale, aren't you?' Carol asked in a low voice, helping Isabella to a sitting position. 'I'm Carol Andrews.'

'I know,' she said, to Carol's surprise. 'They've talked about you a great deal. I knew all about you before you even arrived here.'

'Then you probably know a great deal more than I do. For the moment, though, the most important thing I don't know is how to get these ropes off of you. I need a knife.'

Isabella shook her head. 'There's none

here, I don't think, unless you want to risk going to the kitchen for one. Can't you just untie them?'

Carol looked doubtfully at the knots. 'I'll try. Turn around here, so I can see them better.'

Isabella's hands were tied in front of her and Carol began to fumble with those knots first.

'Have you been tied up like this you came back from Europe?' she asked.

'No, just since shortly before you got here. Until then, they let me move around the house, but everyone watched me like a hawk to be sure I didn't go anywhere unsupervised. But when their guests began to arrive, they brought me in here and tied me so there was no chance of my getting out and finding anyone to tell them what was happening.'

'But why, for Heaven's sake? I mean, why any of it? Why keep you a prisoner? What is all this about, anyway?'

'What did they tell you, exactly?'

'They said they needed someone to impersonate you to make a donation to charity. The World's Children Foundation.

Do you know it?'

'Yes, it's a legitimate organization. But they concocted that scheme after they had made me a prisoner. They wanted to keep me from giving the money away . . . '

'But I did give it away,' Carol interrupted her. 'I saw the check myself. I gave it to Dr. Everson.'

Isabella sighed wearily. 'Yes, I know all about that. But that was only a token gift.'

'A very large token, I'd say.'

'It's a long story.'

'You don't have to tell me now if you don't want to.'

'It's all right. You have a right to hear it. Any luck with those?' She nodded toward the ropes.

'I don't know yet.' In fact, Carol was having no success at all. They had been tied tight and the coarse rope was cutting her fingers, making it difficult to untangle the knots.

'For a long time, I've had a great interest in children,' Isabella said, watching intently as Carol struggled with the knots. 'Something happened once, several years back . . . '

'The accident, with the Winters boy? I know about that.'

'How . . . ?'

'Sorry, go on. I'll tell you my story later.'

Isabella paused before going on, not as if she were hesitant to tell her story, but rather as if she were summoning the strength to do so.

'Well, that accident was like a kind of wakeup call for me. It changed my life. Since then, I've taken a great interest in children's needs, through various foundations and activities. No doubt it will sound strange to you, most people think I'm crazy when I say this, but I have never really enjoyed the wealth I possess. I've felt since . . . since what happened in the past — that the money was only another burden. I've given a great deal of it away over the last several years.'

She seemed to consider that for a moment. 'I suppose if I'm going to be honest, I've been trying to buy off my conscience.'

'A certain amount of guilt can be a good thing. At least if we're frank enough with ourselves to admit we've done wrong, and will try to atone for it. But you mustn't still be beating up on yourself for a youthful mistake. Surely by now you've paid amply.'

Isabella gave her a curious look, but Carol was too occupied with her fruitless efforts with the ropes. After a moment, Isabella went on.

'For almost a year, I had been considering something rather drastic. A few months ago, I finally reached a decision. I told Wilfred that I meant to give the Hale fortune to The World's Children Foundation.'

That brought Carol's head up. 'You mean all of it?'

Isabella managed a wan smile. 'Not quite all of it, as a matter of fact. I meant to set aside a fund for myself to live on, and I intended to settle a modest sum on Wilfred and Minnie. At the time I suggested it, I thought that the sum was a generous one. I actually meant for them to get more than I did. But since I've been here, I've had plenty of time to think about what I had proposed to them. I can understand their shock and their disappointment. Wilfred has always been a good manager for me. I think he's been essentially honest, until now. He's made good investments, and protected my interests. And in return, he and Minnie have been able to live well, just as if the Hale fortune were their own. I've never questioned anything they spent on themselves, or any use they made of the money. Why should I? I had more than I would ever need for myself.

'Unfortunately, at the time I brought this plan of mine up, their reaction to it was quite strong. I think they thought I had gone insane.' She smiled again. 'I suppose you think so too.'

'Not really, but I can understand that they were shocked. It's a rather singular decision, to say the least.'

'Yes. Well, they did threaten to have me declared insane, but that was just an angry threat, and after they had thought about that for a minute or two, they knew how ridiculous that was, it would never have worked. Instead, they simply refused flatly to let me do what I had planned to do. I really don't think at first that they thought of it in terms of keeping me prisoner. They meant — at least, this was how they put it — to protect me from my own foolishness.

'After my announcement, they had come up here, to Hale House. They wanted time to get used to the idea, as they put it. A day or so later, Wilfred called and persuaded me to come up to discuss the matter further. I should have been suspicious when I got here and discovered all the servants had been changed. Everyone that I knew had been dismissed. These people here were all Wilfred's cohorts. I suppose he must have promised each of them a small fortune to go along with his scheme.

'Wilfred and Minnie informed me bluntly that I would have to stay here until I had reached a more reasonable decision. Of course, I became angry myself, I was furious with them for treating me like a child, and I stubbornly refused to reconsider the matter. Worse, I told them that in view of their behavior, I was going to cut them off entirely, with no settlement at all. It was a stupid thing to say, under the circumstances. I should have expected what happened.'

'That's when they made a prisoner of you.'

'Yes.'

Carol thought that Isabella was being overly kind in judging the behavior of her uncle and aunt. Wilfred must have had something of this very sort in mind from the beginning. Why else had he already replaced the servants with the cronies he had hired? But she kept this thought to herself. The woman on the bed had suffered enough already.

'The difficulty was that I had already contacted The World's Children Foundation and made the preliminary arrangements for the presentation dinner. I hadn't told the foundation exactly what I meant to do, so far as giving them the bulk of my fortune, but they knew I was going to give them a gift and that it was going to be generous.

'Wilfred and Minnie had no choice but to go ahead with the dinner and make a generous donation. They may even have thought I would change my thinking and come to agree with them. At any rate, they needed you — or someone enough like me to make the deception believable. And they wanted a houseful of witnesses to see how well they got on with 'me', so that if there were an accident later . . . '

Carol looked up sharply. 'Do you think they were going to . . . to kill you?'

Isabella nodded. She looked as if she might cry just remembering the fact. 'I've no doubt of it. By this time, you see, they had no alternative. They couldn't ever let me go, because they knew I would tell everyone what they had done. They'd have gone to prison. So from their point of view, the only solution was to dispose of me permanently. They've been trying since then to think of an accident that would pass muster. Wilfred has apparently given the impression that this wing is unsafe.'

'Yes. He made sure everyone who was here for the dinner knew that. And what about me?'

'They've been arguing about that, too. Oddly, Wilfred's taken a liking to you, I think. Minnie's been after him to . . . to do something about you, and he's been dragging his feet, sort of.'

'But, if we were both in accidents and people found out that there were two of us, that would be even more suspicious.'

'They meant for you to just disappear, I think. They knew before they hired you that you had no family, and after you arrived here, Wilfred informed your agent that you would be traveling to Europe with them for some months, to work on a film he was producing. They intended eventually to send him a generous fee and a telegram from you, saying that you had given up modeling.'

'And it would have worked,' Carol said, more to herself than to Isabella. She shuddered at the smooth way in which she had been drawn into this web of deceit and danger, virtually unaware until the end that the web had even existed.

'Yes, only something happened to complicate their plans. Or, someone, rather. Some young man, who took a fancy to you . . .'

'Paul. But, you know him. Paul Winters.'

'Winters? You mean that little boy's brother?'

'Yes.'

'How ironic.' Isabella nodded. 'Anyway, he complicated things. If you just disappeared, they were afraid he might ask too many questions. They've been chewing over this since.'

So without even knowing it, Paul had saved her life, at least temporarily. But she was in the same quandary as Isabella. Wilfred and Minnie dared not let either of them go now. Unless she could somehow get herself and Isabella out of here, tonight.

She stood up abruptly. 'It's no use. It will take me hours to get these ropes off this way. I'll have to get a knife and cut them. Look, you'd better lie back down upon the bed, just in case someone looks in on you. We don't want them to suspect. Isn't there some place here I might find a knife?'

Isabella thought for a moment, then: 'Of course, how stupid of me. This room was used for entertaining in the old days. There's a pantry and a bar, over there, that door just at the end of the room. There should be something there you can use.'

Carol found a huge, built-in bar, with shelves of glassware and drawers of gadgets and supplies, and in one of the drawers, a small paring knife, its blade worn thin but still sharp.

She was back to the bed in a minute. 'This should do it,' she said, sawing at the thick ropes with the blade. After a moment, the ropes began to give. A minute more and they fell away, leaving Isabella's hands free.

'Thank Heaven,' Isabella said with a sob of relief. She began to rub her wrists gingerly. They were swollen and cut where the ropes had twisted about them. Carol felt a wave of anger and disgust toward the people who would treat another human being like this. Worse, their victim had been Wilfred's blood relation, and thanks to his position as Isabella's manager, he and Minnie had lived like royalty. She had never in her life wanted anything so much as she wanted to see them receive their just desserts.

A moment more and the ropes were gone from Isabella's ankles as well. Carol stood, tossing the knife aside. 'Do you think you can stand?' she asked, casting an uncertain glance at Isabella's badly swollen ankles.

'I think so. Give me a hand.' With Carol's help, Isabella got to her feet, but her limbs had been unused for too long and she would have fallen if Carol had not held on to her.

'I'll have to go for help,' Carol said, biting her lips.

'No.' Isabella's hand gripped her arm fiercely. 'Please, don't leave me again. I'll go mad if they find me and tie me up again. Give me a moment. I'll be able to make it, I promise.'

Carol thought of what lay before them, of a dangerous and grueling hike down through the woods, and that was only the beginning. Unless they could find a house along the way, they might well have to walk all the way into town. She couldn't remember now how far it had been, but surely it wasn't less than ten miles, maybe more. How could Isabella hope to make it, her strength drained as it was, her limbs so weak she could hardly stand. And they would have to make it before morning — before the others realized they had escaped. Once the cry went up, the hounds would be fast on their trail.

The answer came to her out of the blue. 'The car,' she said. 'If we could unlock the garage, and get it started . . . '

'There are keys in my purse, to the garage and to the car,' Isabella said with a smile that quickly faded. 'Wherever it is,' she added grimly.

'I know where,' Carol said on a triumphant note. 'And the keys are in it. I just saw them myself. Wait here, I'll go get them.'

'Don't leave me,' Isabella begged.

'If I go alone I can get them in a minute and be right back. Wait here, please, it will be better this way.'

She did not give Isabella time to argue, but ran into the hall and up the stairs. In the bedroom upstairs, she grabbed Isabella's purse from the floor and scooped up the billfold as well as the keys — they would very likely need money before this was over and she could not risk going back to her own room for her purse.

Gasping for breath, she ran down again. So intent was she upon speed that she did not think to exercise caution. They needed only a minute or two to make it to the garage. Notwithstanding what Wilfred and Minnie had told her, she was certain the car was there, behind the locked door. Once they drove off in the car, Wilfred and his cohorts would have no way to come after them.

She dashed into the ballroom, holding the keys aloft. 'Got them,' she said aloud. 'Now we can . . .'

She froze in her tracks. Isabella had moved away from the bed and was standing in the center of the vast room, swaying unsteadily. Her frightened eyes rested on Carol for a moment and then swung away.

Mrs. Green, the housekeeper, stood just inside the room, wearing a dressing gown and glowering at her.

10

'I thought I heard something in here,' the housekeeper said, nodding her head grimly. 'It's a good thing I came to investigate.'

Carol sprang toward the open door. The housekeeper moved too, more swiftly than Carol would have expected. The fingers that closed about her wrist were fiercely strong.

'Oh, no you don't,' Mrs. Green said. She threw back her head and yelled, 'Harley! Harley, come in here, quick!'

Carol struggled to break free of her vise-like grip, but Mrs. Green was stronger than she looked. A moment later Harley, in his pajamas, appeared in the doorway.

'What the hell?' He sprang forward, seizing Carol in an embrace from which she could not hope to escape. In a moment, Mrs. Green had grabbed a piece of the rope from the floor and quickly tied Carol's hands together.

'Get the Hales,' the housekeeper

ordered Harley. When he hesitated, she said sharply, 'Go on, I can handle these two now. With her hands tied, she can't do anything, and the other one hasn't got the strength of a newborn baby.'

Harley apparently decided she was right. He went out the door through which Carol had just come. She heard his heavy footsteps pounding up the stairs. He would be returning almost at once, with Wilfred and Minnie.

With a triumphant laugh, Mrs. Green looped another piece of rope about Carol's hands and began to knot it too. She had apparently decided that Isabella represented no threat to her, and she turned her back on her former prisoner.

Isabella, however, saw her chance and seized it. She called upon some last reservoir of strength to move, quickly if unsteadily, across the distance that separated them. As she came, her hand went out to the lamp on the table. She brought it up in one swinging motion and struck the back of Mrs. Green's head with it. The housekeeper's eyes flew wide in a look of astonishment, and then closed.

Slowly, she crumpled, sinking to the floor.

'The knife, hurry,' Carol said. It was on the floor where she had thrown it before. It took a moment for Isabella, her hands still ineffectual, to cut through the rope.

'Come on,' Carol said, grabbing up the keys from where they had fallen in her struggle with Mrs. Green. The light had gone out when Isabella yanked the lamp off the table, but the moon provided enough light for them to see by.

Carol put an arm about Isabella's shoulders to steady her and together they hurried to the French windows. Carol drew the bolt on one of them and threw the door open and they rushed to the terrace outside.

They ran in the direction of the garages, Isabella hobbling as best she could, and Carol half dragging her along, but as they came near to the garages, a light sprang on there.

'The driver,' Isabella said, halting. 'He sleeps out there, in an apartment overheard. He must have Mrs. Green shouting.'

'This way,' Carol said breathlessly, turning her to the left. They ran about the house. She glanced in the direction of the woods, and saw a faint glow of light that seemed to move about, here and then gone. Someone was there. Someone who might help them. But they were so far away — if she screamed, would they even hear? Or care? 'Is there any other way down the hill than by the drive?' she asked as they struggled along. 'A path of some sort?'

'No, not that I know,' Isabella. Her breath was labored and uneven and she was leaning more and more heavily on Carol. The flight down the hillside would be impossible with Isabella as weak as she was.

Isabella stumbled, nearly falling. 'Wait,' she gasped.

The lights suddenly began to come on in the house. Light from an upstairs window threw an elongated rectangle of light across the terrace. Harley had roused Wilfred and Minnie. In a moment they would be in pursuit.

Isabella too had realized flight was impossible for her. 'You'll have to go on without me,' she panted.

'Don't be foolish. Come on, we can make it.'

'I can't, and we both know it. Look, if you get away, they won't dare hurt me. And you can bring help back. It's the only chance we've got.'

Carol hesitated, torn between the natural urge to help Isabella escape too, and her realization that Isabella was right. Alone, there was a possibility, however slim, that she might elude them and escape to bring help. Together they were certain to be caught, and soon.

'Go on, run,' Isabella said, giving her a weak push.

'I'll bring someone,' Carol said, deciding. 'Tell them that. Promise them nothing will happen if they just don't carry this any further.'

From inside, Minnie's voice cried, 'They've gotten away. Lord, we have got to catch them.'

Carol had no time to make plans or think what she could do. She gave a last, tearful look at Isabella. Then she began to run.

She had almost reached the front of the house when from inside she heard Wilfred's voice, loud and alarmed, carrying easily through the stillness of the night.

'You go after them that way,' he cried. 'I'll head them off in the front. Shoot them if you have to.'

Carol came to a halt in the shadows. Isabella was already out of sight behind her. She knew Isabella would offer no resistance. They would not have to shoot her.

But there was no hope now that she could get across the parking area and down the drive, out of sight, before Wilfred saw her. He would kill her if he must, even shoot her in the back, to prevent her escape. At this point, it had come down to their lives or hers and she had no doubt which he would choose.

'You won't have to shoot,' Isabella said in the distance behind her, speaking clearly. 'Here I am.'

Carol flattened herself against the wall of the house, her thoughts racing wildly.

'Here's one of them,' Minnie called. 'Where's that other one?'

Carol heard Isabella laugh loudly. 'You're too late,' she said, 'she's reached the woods already. You'll never find her now.'

'The devil we won't,' Minnie said. 'Take her inside, Harley.'

Carol's hand went out and touched glass — the French windows of the drawing room. Scarcely thinking what she was going to do, she pushed against them. They were bolted from the inside, but the bolts were flimsy.

She held the handle so that the door would not crash open and shoved hard with her shoulder against the door framing. The bolt gave with a cracking sound she hoped they would not hear, and the door opened. She slipped inside, pushing the door shut.

A moment later, Wilfred ran past the window. He held a flashlight in one hand, shining it down on the ground, and in his other hand he held a gun.

Carol felt as if ghostly hands were at her throat, strangling her. She could hardly breathe and her heart was crashing violently against her ribs.

She heard Wilfred say, 'I didn't see her. She didn't come this way.'

'She was too fast,' Minnie replied. 'The other one said she made it into the woods.'

'Damn those bitches,' Wilfred swore. The words sound incongruous in his elegantly clipped voice. 'We'll have to go after them.'

'I'll get the car,' another voice said. It was McCullogh, the chauffeur. He had joined the chase by this time.

Carol stood in the darkness of the drawing room, trembling and trying to think what she could possibly do. The phones were useless. There was no one in the house from whom she could expect help or even sympathy. Escape was cut off. In time they would realize she had not made it as far as the woods, and the only other place she could be was in the house.

Outside there was a flurry of commotion. She heard the garage door thrown open, car doors slamming, and the roar as the engine came to life. Twin beams of light suddenly shot across the drive.

Minnie was in command now, barking orders like a military officer. 'You stay here with that damned princess,' she yelled, her tone one that brooked no argument. 'Harley, you and Wilfred start down the hill on either side of the driveway. That's the only way she could have gone. McCullogh and me will go down the hill part way and work our way back up. She couldn't have gotten too far unless she was flying.'

Carol ticked them off in her mind. It was Mrs. Green, then, who was left behind with Isabella — the others were all accounted for. The housekeeper was not so formidable a threat on her own. Certainly she would not expect Carol still to be inside the house. With surprise on her side, Carol might be able to overpower her. After that, she would have to think about how to get away from the others. Without the car, and with Isabella so weak, she could not imagine how that would be possible, but she must make the attempt.

She was standing just inside the French doors, leaning against the glass. She had not even thought of the curve of the driveway as it came about the house. The lights of the car began to move, growing brighter. Then, suddenly, they were swinging about as the car turned. There was no time for her to move aside. She barely realized what was happening.

The headlights fell full upon her, gleaming through the glass.

She jumped aside, hiding behind the drapes. Outside, there was a shower of gravel as the car stopped abruptly. After a pause, Minnie said, too loudly, 'No, wait, I just thought of something.'

It was a ruse. They had seen her, and intended to surprise her. She dropped to a crouched position and moved past the sofa, running stooped down to avoid the glare of the headlights that still shone through the French doors.

At the hall, she stood and ran as if the demons of hell were after her. It was no good to think that escape was impossible, no good to remember their guns or Wilfred's order to shoot. This was the moment of elemental struggle, when she must do the only thing left for her to do — run for her life!

Her lungs felt as if they might burst. She ran with all the strength her young body could summon and yet it seemed to take an eternity to reach the front door and fling it open. Her terrified brain screamed for her feet to move faster but they might have been made of lead, so clumsy did they feel. She heard sobs of terror and realized they were her own.

Like a frightened deer she half ran, half stumbled down the front steps. She nearly fell as she raced across the parking square, heading not for the drive, but straight for the woods. They were her only hope now of escape.

An automobile engine roared to life, coming closer. Headlights swept over her, blinding her. She tried to turn aside, but her foot slipped in the gravel and she went tumbling and sprawling to the ground. Sharp stones cut into the flesh of her hands.

She saw the headlights rushing down upon her. In her terror, she seemed to see them multiplied, doubled as it were. They seemed to surround her, to come at her from every side.

'They're going to run me down,' she thought. She screamed and her scream blended with the crash of ripping metal and the splatter of flying gravel.

Stones showered down upon her and the lights went out — but no car struck her.

'Isabella,' someone cried, and in her confusion she thought it was Paul's voice. Someone was running toward her, footsteps crunching loudly in the gravel, but she had no strength left with which to flee. It was hopeless. It was over. She lay and cried helplessly into her hands.

Someone seized her in strong arms, lifting her. She opened her eyes and found herself looking up into Paul's handsome, frightened face.

She tried to say something but she couldn't speak for the sobs wracking her body, making her tremble. He picked her up, lifting her from the ground easily as if she weighed nothing at all. Her head fell wearily against his chest, and he whispered, 'I told you I'd come back for you.'

★   ★   ★

The rest was a blur. She was only dimly aware of the men all about her, strangers, some of them in uniforms and wearing badges. But for now, she cared only for the arms that held her, carrying her into the house.

Later, when calm had settled over Hale House and Paul had held her gently and whispered things to her that were wonderful to hear, and she had sipped some brandy to revive her, there came a time for explanations.

'My hesitation almost cost you your life,' Paul said.

He and Carol and Isabella, and a man whom Carol now knew to be the local sheriff, were in the library, which, only a short time before, had belonged to Wilfred. The others had all gone away. Wilfred and Minnie, Harley and McCullogh, and Mrs. Green, looking very grim, had been escorted to a variety of cars by a number of serious looking men in sheriff's uniforms.

'I thought it was Michael Forrest,' Carol said, 'standing out there and watching the house.' She saw Isabella flinch a little at the mention of her fiancé. They had already heard of the shallow grave in the woods that had been

Wilfred's final solution to the problem of Mr. Forrest. The grave was only a few yards away from where Mr. Forrest's car had been hidden. Carol had nearly stumbled upon it herself on her walk in the woods.

'I'm sorry,' Carol said, reaching over to pat Isabella's hand.

Isabella smiled wanly. 'It's all right. I already knew what they had done, you know. They told me that he'd been here looking for me, and I said he was going to rescue me, and Minnie laughed and told me what had happened to him. By then she had already made up her mind, of course, that I had to die too, or she'd never have admitted it.'

'I just couldn't get it out of my head that something was very wrong here,' Paul said, picking up the thread of his story again. 'I left here that final day, but halfway to town I turned around and started back, and I saw that butler — Harley, is that his name? — drive Forrest's car into the woods. That struck me as really peculiar. My first idea was that Forrest had decided to stay on. I may as well be honest, I was jealous. I thought I had been deceived.'

He gave Carol an apologetic look. 'I was angry. I came back today thinking I would come right up here and demand an explanation from you. But by the time I had made the long drive back, I had begun to wonder about that car. I couldn't figure out, if Forrest was staying here, why it was necessary to hide his car in the woods. Who were they hiding it from? So I went to have another look at where it had been, and it was gone. But I saw something else. It looked just about like what it was.'

'A grave,' Carol said.

'Yes. I couldn't imagine what else it might be. I didn't know what to think then. I left my car there and walked up the hill. I thought I wanted to give you a chance to tell me what was going on. I waited, thinking I'd catch you outside, alone, hoping for a chance to talk to you privately, but the only ones I saw were Wilfred and Minnie.'

'I had gone upstairs by that time,' Carol said. 'I saw you — I didn't know it was you, actually, I thought it was Mr. Forrest. But by the time I came down, you had already left.'

'I had come to the conclusion that, if that really was a grave in the woods, which was certainly what it appeared to be, it meant one of two things. You were in on something pretty rotten, or you were innocent and in danger. That's when I decided to go for the sheriff.'

'It took a long time to convince me,' the sheriff said, a bit ruefully, 'or we'd have been up here a lot sooner. I didn't really believe any of this until I saw that grave myself. When I did, I had my boys start digging. As soon as we saw what was in it . . . well, that's when we decided we had better get up here fast. And we pulled up just in time to see them try to run you down.'

Carol shuddered as she thought again of how close she had come to death in that moment before the sheriff, in his car, had deliberately collided with the other car.

'I'm the one who is really to blame,' Carol said. 'None of this would have come about if I hadn't willingly been party to a deception.'

'No, they'd have just found somebody else if you hadn't agreed,' Isabella said. 'By that time, they were committed to their schemes. I was their prisoner. Once they had done that, there was nothing they could do but go ahead with their plans.'

'Besides, your motives were good,' Paul said. 'And you did do a lot of good, actually. At the very least, you helped me free myself of a burden of hate I had been carrying around inside myself for a long time.'

'I wonder if I would have acquitted myself as well,' Isabella said. 'You seem to have defended me quite marvelously.'

'I'm sure you would have accomplished the same thing,' Carol said. 'Maybe even with the same results. I think Paul's sudden love for me really belonged to you. I think it sprang in part from the violent hate he had felt for so long.'

Paul, sitting on the sofa next to her, put an arm about her gently. 'No,' he said, softly but firmly. 'On that subject, let there be no confusion. The woman I love is the woman you are, not the one you pretended to be. I was confused, and be-wildered, but I knew when I saw you, and when I kissed you, that I had found some-thing I had been searching for all my life.

'Did you think for a single moment that I would just let you go? I didn't know what the trouble was here, or why you had acted so strangely, but I knew that I would never again be able to live without you.'

She made no reply. Nor was he waiting for one. His mouth found hers and at the touch of his lips she forgot the others who were present in the room, forgot the fear she had suffered. No further explanations or apologies were necessary.

He and his love were hers. And not even Isabella Hale, with all her millions, was as rich as she was in that knowledge.

THE END

We do hope that you have enjoyed reading this large print book.

Did you know that all of our titles are available for purchase?

We publish a wide range of high quality large print books including:
Romances, Mysteries, Classics
General Fiction
Non Fiction and Westerns

Special interest titles available in large print are:
The Little Oxford Dictionary
Music Book, Song Book
Hymn Book, Service Book

Also available from us courtesy of Oxford University Press:
Young Readers' Dictionary
(large print edition)
Young Readers' Thesaurus
(large print edition)

For further information or a free brochure, please contact us at:
Ulverscroft Large Print Books Ltd.,
The Green, Bradgate Road, Anstey,
Leicester, LE7 7FU, England.
Tel: (00 44) 0116 236 4325
Fax: (00 44) 0116 234 0205

TEACH YOURSELF TREACHERY

John Burke

Rachel Petersen's husband had drowned in Holland — so who is the man who appears at her house and claims to be that husband, substantiating his claim with a passport and detailed recollections of their brief married life? From the moment the stranger calling himself Erik Flemming Petersen steps through the door, there is no peace for Rachel. She determines to unravel the tangled threads of the mystery — only to find they are more tightly woven than she could have suspected . . .

PIT AND THE PENDULUM

John Gregory Betancourt

Peter 'Pit Bull' Keller is a ruined man . . . A *wunderkind* at a Wall Street investment bank, his constantly racing mind started his downfall — a nervous breakdown, caused by working twenty-hour days, seven days a week. Then, just as he was beginning to pull himself together mentally, a taxi ran a red light and hit him, crippling him permanently. But despite his dependence on alcohol and pain-killers, Peter's exceptional intelligence remain intact — as many criminals find to their cost . . .

THE RETURN OF SHERLOCK HOLMES

Ernest Dudley

Though Professor Moriarty has perished at the Reichenbach Falls, Sherlock Holmes must still pit his wits against his old and deadly enemies — the malevolent blackmailer Charles Augustus Milverton, and the murderous Colonel Sebastian Moran . . . In this collection the author also gives us another of his own fictional creations: the sardonic Martin Brett — a more modern equivalent of the great detective — in four further ingenious stories of murder and mystery.

MURDER IN MANUSCRIPT

Gerald Verner

The murder of a mysterious recluse in Barnet supplies Mr. Budd with one of the most difficult cases of his career. What is the connection between Jonathan Haines, the murdered man, and the typist who is found murdered later that same day? Mr. Budd, with the assistance of crime reporter Bob Hopkins and the melancholy Sergeant Leek, succeeds in piecing together all the fragments of the puzzle — but not until the stout superintendent has suffered the most terrifying experience of his life . . .

THE TWISTED TONGUES

John Burke

A wartime traitor who broadcast from Germany is finally released from prison. Nobody wanted to listen to him during the war and nobody wants to listen to him now. But he intends to be heard, and when he begins to write his memoirs for a newspaper, old ghosts stir uneasily and it becomes a race against time: will he reveal the truth behind the smug respectability of men in high places before they find a means of silencing him forever?

ANGEL DOLL

Arlette Lees

It's the dark days of the Great Depression, and former Boston P.D. detective Jack Dunning is starting over after losing both his wife and his job to the bottle. Fresh off the Greyhound, he slips into The Blue Rose Dance Hall — and falls hard for a beautiful dime-a-dance girl, Angel Doll. But then Angel shoots gangster Axel Teague and blows town on the midnight train to Los Angeles . . .